". . . I came up from a dive and was treading water when Bob Pamperin came high out of the water about sixty feet from me, and screamed 'Help me.' I swam toward Bob and, in looking ahead, could see nothing. After swimming about one-half of the way to the spot where Bob Pamperin had shot out of the water, I submerged and there, soon, about five feet away, I saw Bob's face, chest, and arms; the area below the torso was obscured by reddish brown, murky fluid; the lower part of Bob's body appeared to be in the mouth of an enormous, heavy-bodied white shark . . ."

—From one of the accounts of shark attack in this book.

SHARKS: ATTACKS ON MAN

George A. Llano

tempo books

GROSSET & DUNLAP
PUBLISHERS   NEW YORK

To my wife
Barbara Pray
who kept the
home fires
burning

"The right of a shark to live after his lights is precisely that of other animated creatures . . . They belong to one of the world's few really old families. Therefore, if there is anything in priority of possession, the sharks have a much better right to kill us than we have to kill them for they had been a long established race ages and ages before we appeared . . . adjusted to our environment with such a close approach to perfection that there had been no necessity for them to change either their structure or their habits in all the passing eons. They preceded us here and the chances are that they will survive us. We hate them because we fear them."

—an Editorial in the *New York Times* July 19, 1916.

CONTENTS

CONTENTS

SHARKS

ATTACKS
ON
MAN

INTRODUCTION

A human being in the water is usually so helpless against sharks, and the consequences of shark attack are so gruesome and horrible to contemplate, that nobody exposed to the possibility of it can banish it from his mind and whoever has survived an attack can never forget it. Mere statistics are no comfort, for shark attack is always a possibility to be dreaded, no matter how remote and unlikely.

Knowledge of the behavior of sharks towards humans in the water or on rafts has long been largely speculative, and the literature on the subject, both popular and technical, is full of contradictory evidence and opinions. It still seems that the best evidence is the first-hand accounts of those who have encountered sharks.

Very few accounts describe the sharks involved in enough detail to identify them accurately. To the man in the water the specific identity of the shark swimming near him is of little importance. Though some of the largest sharks, such as the whale shark and the basking shark, are plankton feeders not able to prey on man, size is the main concern when a shark is encountered. Any shark large enough to hurt a man must be considered dangerous, and that means any shark more than 3 or 4 feet in length. In fact, the International Shark Attack File credits three eighteen-inch-long lemon sharks with an attack.

There are about 250 species of sharks which are grouped by scientists into about 20 families. These are found in all seas except in Antarctic waters, and quite frequently in brackish and fresh water. The largest sharks, the whale and basking sharks, may grow to 50 feet and weigh several tons. These harmless giant sharks feed on micro-algae and small organisms which are strained from the sea water through specialized gill rakers. Basking sharks take in sea water through their mouths at the rate of 2,000 gallons per hour and eject it through their large gills. Another large and inoffensive shark is the sleeper or Greenland shark found in Arctic seas. There are many other smaller sharks which are harmless. Some, like the dog-fish shark, travel in large schools.

The sharks that have the teeth, jaws, and

instincts necessary for a rapacious way of life, and that have been incriminated as man-eaters, are members of the "requiem" family. These include the mackerel, white shark, whaler shark, tiger shark, blue shark, sea shark, blue pointer or mako, grey nurse, hammerhead, and white- and black-tipped sharks.

The great white shark, the largest after the basking, whale, and Greenland sharks, is credited with being the most ferocious monster of the deep. It is a heavily built, fast-swimming, far-ranging fish of the open ocean. Savagely aggressive, it has been known to attack boats. One authority describes it as having "a vast greediness after human flesh." The fact is that when it ranges inshore, it becomes a killer, striking haphazardly at widely separated areas. Coppleson in his book *Shark Attack* attributes these incidents to long-range cruising rogue sharks. Over the last fifty years, white sharks have made terrifying attacks on bathers on the U.S. coast—in 1936 in Buzzards Bay, Massachusetts (at the foot of Cape Cod) and, since 1952, at several localities off southern California.

There are other dangerous sharks in the "requiem" group. The origin of the name is lost in antiquity, but it is certainly appropriate. One of its members is the mako. Like the white shark, it is large, aggressive, and widely distributed. It is a vigorous leaper, much hunted as a game fish and the favorite sport fish of Zane Grey. Another member is the tiger shark, a fish of ill repute from the Antilles to the Antipodes. Australian pearl divers consider it the most vicious of all the sharks, and it is also greatly feared in the West Indies. The tiger, a sneaking scavenger, pursues its prey into the shallowest waters; it lurks around docks and haunts ships at anchor. It is without doubt the commonest large shark in the tropics. It feeds on anything, with little regard for edibility, and has been known to turn cannibal on its peers in size and ferocity.

Another member of the family with a disagreeable reputation is the lemon shark. Like the tiger, it hangs around docks and ships. The lemon also is prone to run into brackish bays. This species is suspected of having been the culprit in a series of shark attacks on bathers in South Carolina waters between 1919 and 1933, and further south to the Florida beaches.

By means of tagging returns, we are now finding that large sharks on the Eastern Coast of the United States move regularly between

New Jersey and Florida. Some movements may be as much as 1,000 miles in over 100 days; other records show as little movement as two miles in about 50 days.

The blue shark (*Prionace glauca*) a representative of another genus in the requiem family, has had a bad reputation among sailors from time immemorial. It is credited with 9 fatal attacks by the International Shark Attack File; and its persistent attentions gave many a life-raft party a bad time during World War II. With its brilliant blue back and snow-white belly, this species is the most conspicuous and identifiable of all the sharks; most other sharks are drab gray or brown.

The genus with the most numerous population in the requiem family is *Carcharhinus*. Its species are found in all warm seas up to the 40th parallel. They range over the open ocean and in brackish and fresh waters. At least three species in the group live in fresh water; one of them inhabits land-locked Lake Nicaragua and makes it a feared body of water.

Incidentally, the common U. S. notion that sharks are a menace only on seacoasts is wrong. Not only are there inland species but marine sharks have been known to travel far upstream into continental and inland rivers. They have been reported in the Amazon; in the Senegal and Zambezi rivers of Africa; in the Ganges, Tigris and Euphrates of Asia; in the fresh waters of Malaya and Siam; in the upper Sarawak of Borneo; in the Fitzroy and Margaret rivers of Western Australia, and in a number of other places. The Ganges River shark has attacked pilgrims during their sacred bathing in the river and its tributaries. In Iran 27 shark attacks, half of them fatal, were reported during the period 1941 to 1949 in the Karun River near the town of Ahwaz, 90 miles from the Persian Gulf.

Sharks are found in all oceans and seas of the world. Why they are absent south of the Antarctic Circle is anyone's guess. Many species live and feed only at considerable depths. Others remain constantly at higher levels, and it is these "cruising sharks," which hunt near the surface, and whose high dorsal fins frequently project above the water, that come most frequently in contact with man.

While by no means rare in high latitudes— several kinds are common in the Arctic—only those inhabiting warmer waters are implicated in human tragedies. Shark attacks on humans are restricted, by and large, to the seas and oceans between 40° N. and 40° S. latitude. One reason for this may be that people are seldom exposed to sharks in frigid waters. Another reason is that the shallow water and surface sharks as a group are more abundant and more active where water temperatures are 68° F. (20° C.) or higher. In fact, the first specimen of the great white shark north of Washington State was not found until 1961. The authentic records of shark attacks north of 40° N. are generally limited to the warm summer months. The evidence shows the sharks in warmer waters to be far more aggressive than those in temperate waters. The record also shows an increasing number of attacks at higher latitudes—as predicted by Llano in 1957.

The normal diet of nearly all sharks consists of living animals. All have voracious appetites, and many will turn scavenger. They may travel singly or in packs, and are guided to their food by sound, scent and sight in that order.

Cruising sharks apparently investigate all floating objects, and are prone to strike at injured or helpless animals, although healthy prey are their normal food. Their sense of smell is highly developed, and it is generally conceded that the presence of blood in the water excites them. They are extremely sensitive to vibrations transmitted through the water, and abnormal impulses such as those made by a fish fighting against a hook and line or by the struggles of an injured or dying animal or a poorly coordinated swimmer, (and from a shark's point of view, all humans must look like dreadful swimmers) even the rapid, excited progress of another shark approaching food will draw them from a greater distance than the scent of blood. They are known to be drawn by unusual noises such as underwater explosions.

A popular fallacy often encountered is that a shark must turn on its side or back in order to bite. Sharks with mouths well back under the head may turn partly on their sides to reach their prey on the surface, but they do not have to. When a shark moves to strike, it arrives mouth first, and since the front of it is all mouth, it can bite a man from almost any position. The jaws of the great white shark and other open-ocean species are so far forward that the animals can bite floating objects easily without twisting on their sides.

Biting habits vary with dentition and feeding methods. Man-eating sharks are frequently described as capable of severing a man's body or limbs at a snap. In the case of the 1959 incident at La Jolla, the great shark took Pamperin whole. Shark teeth are adapted to shearing; additional force is brought to bear by strong body motions, including an avulsive rotation of the body, or a twisting movement of the head and body with or without a rapid vibration of the head. At the moment of striking, the jaws are protruded, erecting and locking the teeth in position; since the upper jaw is immovable, the lower jaw provides the biting action. Dusky sharks about 8 feet long have a tested biting pressure of about 18 metric tons per square inch. White sharks have reputedly broken chain with a parting strength of 3,800 pounds.

Shark bites are typically half-moon incisions, often with good impressions of the smaller teeth left in the untorn flesh. A remarkable aspect of shark bite is the high percentage of those who have survived being bitten who are unable to recall feeling any pain from the bite at the time.

Sharks also injure by means of striking with the leading edge of their pectoral fins or hitting with their heads. These bumping tactics are very disconcerting, and are difficult to explain. Pectoral fin blows leave a characteristic straight-line imprint, while rubbing of the shagreen skin can rasp the skin off a man's body.

Sharks segregate pretty much by size. This appears to be a matter for survival, since large sharks feed on smaller ones. Thus a natural nipping order is established. In general, however, all sharks, regardless of size, keep clear of the hammerhead, whose rudder-like head gives it a swimming advantage over other sharks. Sharks may hunt and attack singly, but in some incidents, survivors have had to cope with several at a time. Small sharks are particularly apt to occur in schools and to attack in numbers. They circle their prey, appearing out of nowhere and frequently rising swiftly from below. The feeding behavior is intensified by numbers and rapid to-and-fro swimming when three or more sharks appear in the presence of food. The swimming movement increases from aimless swimming to tight circling to rapid crisscross passes. This often intensifies into a "shark frenzy," when shark turns on shark and injured ones are devoured regardless of size.

Sharks apparently feed at all hours, but may abstain from food for varying periods. In captivity, they may refuse food altogether. Large males may feed very little during courtship, and gravid females on nursery grounds appear to be similarly inhibited. Darkness increases the chances for an attack since sharks are then more active inshore. Different species vary considerably in this respect. Commercial fishermen have found some kinds of sharks to be more active and more easily caught at night. In open-sea survival narratives, the preponderance of shark sightings and attacks occurred during daylight, a high percentage of them in the late afternoon. According to *Shark Attack: A Program of Data Reduction and Analysis*, which treats 1165 of the more than 1652 attacks on record in the International Shark Attack File, inshore attacks occur with greatest frequency at the times when most swimmers would be expected to be present. There is a morning rise to a peak at approximately 11 a.m., then a falling off until a new, higher peak occurs in midafternoon (3-4 p.m.), again falling off to low numbers around nightfall. These data confirm Coppleson's analysis in *Shark Attack* (1958), which was principally based on attacks along Australian beaches during the Australian summer. According to Coppleson, most incidents occurred between 10 a.m. and 6 p.m.

THE
UNITED
STATES

CALIFORNIA

On December 7, 1952, at about 2 p.m. 17-year-old Barry Wilson was attacked by a large shark while he was swimming at Pacific Grove, California. The water was cool (55 degrees) and murky. Visibility was only 6 or 8 feet. A surf was running to a height of about 8 feet.

Wilson and his friend Brookner Brady Jr. were swimming about 25 yards offshore in 30 feet of water when John C. Bassford, on the shore, saw Wilson jerk himself around in the water and peer in all directions. A look of terror crossed Wilson's face. Then Bassford saw the shark approaching Wilson. It struck from the front and heaved him almost out of the water. Wilson, both hands on the shark's back, was pushing to free himself when he toppled sideways and was pulled under. Soon blood welled up from below and spread into a six-foot circle on the surface. In a few seconds Wilson surfaced, screaming for help and beating the water with his hands. The shark reappeared, swam by very close to Wilson, showing its back, and returned in another pass before disappearing—for the time being.

Meanwhile, Bassford had shouted to warn Brady to get away. Brady swam at once to Wilson, and had towed him about 75 feet when they were met by four members of the Sea Otter Club, a skindiving group, who had come out to help. They had an inner tube, and started to get Wilson into it. But the body gave a sudden lunge; one of the divers was so sure that someone had pushed Wilson that he looked around to see who had done it. No one was there; he glanced down, and saw the tail end of the shark disappearing.

Once Wilson was in the tube the group set off for shore, on a swim that must have lasted twenty minutes. Whenever the swimmers stopped to resettle the body, which kept slipping from the tube, the shark was apt to reappear. It seemed to the swimmers to come closer when they stopped, and to stay further away when they were moving.

Wilson was pronounced dead upon his arrival on shore, and in fact he had probably died in a very few minutes. The femoral artery had been severed, and the right leg savaged deeply. At least four bites were probably inflicted, and the shark had probably attacked

Wilson at least once while he was surrounded by the other swimmers.

The shark responsible was probably a great white, judging from the descriptions of witnesses and the toothmarks. Estimates of its length varied from 8 to 15 feet.

On May 7, 1959, Albert Kogler and Shirley O'Neill, both 18-year-old students at San Francisco State College, went for a late afternoon dip at Baker Beach, just west of the Golden Gate Bridge. It was an unusually warm day, with a temperature of 80 degrees.

The two were swimming fifty yards from shore when Miss O'Neill heard Kogler scream.

"I turned around and saw this big gray thing flap up into the air. I don't know if it was a fin or a tail. I knew it was some kind of fish.

"There was a thrashing in the water and I knew he was struggling with it. It must have been pretty big.

"He screamed again: " 'It's a shark ... get out of here!'

"I started swimming back. I swam a few strokes, but then I thought to myself: " 'I can't just leave him here.'

"I was scared. I didn't know what to do,

but I knew I couldn't leave him. I turned around and took a couple of strokes back.

"He just kept screaming and screaming ... it was a horrible scream ... He was shouting: " 'Help me, help me!' "

Miss O'Neill reached for his hand, "but when I pulled I could see that his arm was just hanging by a thread."

"Finally I told him: 'The only way I can help you is if you lie still on your back ... lie back and relax.' He did that. If he hadn't, I never would have been able to get him back.

"He didn't scream after that. The pain must have been awful but he didn't complain."

Once on the beach, Miss O'Neill, a Roman Catholic, baptized Kogler with sea water.

Just before he became unconscious he whispered: "I love God and I love my mother and I love my father. Oh God, help me. God help me."

He died two hours later.

W. I. Follett, curator of fishes at the California Academy of Sciences, identified the shark as a great white from the evidence of the tooth marks.

Miss O'Neill was awarded a silver medal by

the Carnegie Hero Fund Commission for her assistance to Kogler.

On June 14, 1959, Robert Lyell Pamperin and his friend Gerald H. Lehrer went skin diving for abalone off La Jolla, California.

Lehrer's sworn statement of the events that afternoon follows:

"That on Sunday June 14, 1959, about 5:00 p.m., the affiant [Lehrer] and Robert L. Pamperin equipped themselves with [swim] fins, face plates, abalone irons, an inflated inner tube and burlap bag and entered the Pacific Ocean from Alligator Rock, a point about one hundred yards from the Cove in La Jolla, California; that the affiant and Robert L. Pamperin swam out about one hundred and fifty feet in a northerly direction from Alligator Rock in search of abalone; that in this area the water is about twenty or thirty feet deep and the bottom is characterized by ledges of rock covered with eel-grass and sandy bottom between the ledges; that the affiant and Robert L. Pamperin are [were] thoroughly familiar with the area, having dived for abalone near Alligator Rock on many occasions in the past year; that the water was unusually warm and moderately clear.

"That the affiant came up from a dive and was treading water when Bob Pamperin came high out of the water about sixty feet from the affiant, and screamed "Help me." His face plate was off, but his abalone-iron was tied around his wrist. The affiant swam toward Bob and, in looking ahead, affiant could see nothing. After swimming about one-half of the way to the spot where Bob Pamperin had shot out of the water, the affiant submerged and there [soon], about five feet away, the affiant saw Bob's face, chest and arms; that the area below the torso was obscured by reddish brown, murky fluid, which the affiant recognized as blood; that the lower part of Bob's body appeared to be in the mouth of an enormous, heavy bodied white shark, which was on its back; that although the lower part of Bob's body was obscured with blood, it was apparent to affiant the legs and lower portion of Bob's body was in the shark's mouth. The affiant could see Bob's face clearly and the affiant is certain that Robert L. Pamperin was dead.

"The affiant could do nothing for Robert L. Pamperin and had no equipment with which to attack the shark.

"The affiant surfaced and swam toward

shore, looking downward and backward toward the shark; that other swimmers were swimming to the area and affiant warned them back, and affiant was helped onto Alligator Rock.

Affiant cannot accurately estimate the length of the shark because of the blood around the shark's mouth and the lower part of Robert L. Pamperin's body obscured the head and snout, but affiant ... [believes] the length to be about twenty feet.

"As the affiant swam toward shore after the attack, he saw Bob's [swim] fin floating away. Prior to the attack, the affiant saw no evidence of the shark.

"Affiant is of the opinion that Robert Lyell Pamperin was dead when affiant saw his lower torso in the jaws of the shark, and affiant is of the opinion that the shark devoured his remains as affiant swam toward shore."

Another sworn affidavit was that of William F. Abitz of San Diego, who stated ". . . that on June 14, 1959 at about 5:00 p.m. the affiant in company with his wife and mother was picnicking on the grass in the park at the La Jolla Cove; that affiant heard someone shout that a swimmer was in trouble; that affiant ran out on Alligator Rock; that affiant observed, from this point, a swimmer about 100 to 150 feet away (the affiant later learned that this man was Gerald H. Lehrer) swimming around in a confused manner, shouting "a shark got my buddy." The affiant swam out to Gerald H. Lehrer and helped him onto a rock about two feet below the surface of the water [ten yards off Alligator Rock]; affiant observed that Lehrer's face was ashen white and his eyes were wide with terror; that Lehrer wanted to go back to his friend, but affiant could see no sign of Lehrer's buddy and observed that Lehrer, due to shock, was in no condition to be of any help; that affiant persuaded Lehrer to swim to Alligator Rock, about 100 feet away, and affiant swam beside Lehrer to help, if needed; that Lehrer swam in an erratic fashion constantly changing his style and saying that he wanted to go back to his buddy.

"After helping Lehrer to shore, affiant observed that Lehrer was suffering from shock; his face was still ashen white and his eyes were enormously large, and in relating the shark attack on Robert L. Pamperin, Lehrer was coherent but horrified.

"While swimming out to Lehrer, the affiant

saw a dark shadowy substance in the water, which may have been blood or may have been the reflection of shadowy rocks. The affiant never did see Pamperin or a shark."

Conrad Limbaugh, head diver at Scripps Institution of Oceanography, charged with investigating all such tragedies, reported to the Institution as follows:

"Shortly after the incident, I arrived at the scene and observed a number of persons skin and SCUBA diving over the area where the victim was last seen. . . .

"Approximately nine volunteer divers put in a total estimated four and one-half man-hours SCUBA diving in the immediate vicinity of the attack. The water visibility was about 20′ and the temperature was 68 degrees . . . No evidence of the victim was found.

"Mr. Harold B. MacDuffy, piloting a Coast Guard helicopter over the area an hour or so afterward, saw a blue [swim] fin floating, but didn't recover it. He reported seeing a seal but did not see any sharks . . ."

Limbaugh interviewed Lehrer and reported back to Scripps: . . . "[Lehrer] swam toward him. The victim disappeared beneath the water. The partner looked down through a mask which corrects for the magnification of the water and saw the victim in the jaws of a shark, estimated to be 20 feet in length.

"The shark was three-fourths upside down on a sand-patch. The victim was held between the shark's jaws about his waist; his legs were not visible. The shark was jerking its head and lashing its tail. . . . This behavior might be expected of a shark that doesn't saw its food with broad serrated teeth, but holds it with its teeth and swallows the prey entire.

"The partner described the tail as having a much larger upper lobe than lower lobe and indicated that the teeth were only about one and one-fourth inches long (relatively small). The width of the shark was indicated by his hands to be about 32 to 34 inches, indicating a relatively slim shark. The shark [was described as having] . . . a white ventral surface which graded to an even gray above; there were no blotches or other markings. The partner didn't notice any of the fins nor the head.

"He [Lehrer] approached the shark, hoping to frighten it away. The shark didn't move and the witness felt that he couldn't help the victim. He backed away noting that the abalone iron was still around the victim's wrist . . ."

"Prior to the incident, several conditions may have contributed to the attack. The presence of unusually warm water during the past three years has probably permitted or attracted warm water sharks into southern California waters. One day before the accident a beaked whale came ashore at La Jolla Shores approximately 800 yards from the scene of the tragedy. Some blood from this mammal may have caused the shark to remain in this general area.

"Several yellowtail had been speared in the attack area less than two hours prior to the incident. Approximately one hour before the tragedy, a sailor lacerated himself on a rock and lost considerable blood . . .

"Approximately 600 yards west of the cove there is a small rookery of harbor seals. Possibly the shark was after one of these. The fact that the victim had taken two abalone suggests the possibility that he may have scratched himself and lost a little blood which could have attracted the shark . . ."

In July of that year, another attack occurred at La Jolla. Verne Fleet, a 25-year-old lifeguard, was skin-diving 300 yards from the site of Pamperin's death when his spear line got tangled. As he surfaced to straighten it out, he "felt a tingling sensation" on his thigh.

"I rolled in the water and brushed it away with one hand. Then I saw it was a hammer-head."

The 6-foot shark swam around him in lazy circles. When he headed for shore, it swam away. A 10-foot length of fishing line trailed from its mouth.

Mr. Fleet sustained fifteen tooth punctures on his upper left thigh. The lower edge of his swimming trunks were shredded.

In the same week, off La Jolla Cove, the boat of fisherman James L. Randles, jr., was attacked by a 10-foot "white shark." The shark snatched some fish hung over the side. Mr. Randles reported that he fired four pistol shots and thrust a metal spear into the shark's head before it swam away.

In November, 1959, Duffie Fryling, a 21-year-old lifeguard, went skindiving for lobster about 75 yards offshore from Paradise Cove, near Malibu, California.

"I know that area very well and it somehow seemed too quiet that day as I swam out," he said. "There was something ominous about the quiet—or maybe I was just having a hunch.

It was about 1:30 in the afternoon; no other swimmers were around.

"I saw a pretty big school of sharks swimming together in the same direction, but this didn't seem too unusual. There are always a few around."

Fryling said he realized he was in danger when he neared a clump of kelp and saw that blood was in the water. "About 25 feet ahead of me I saw a surging, swirling chaos of blue sharks," he said. There were about 15 sharks, he added.

It looked like two or three of the sharks had been wounded, he said. He tried to swim back to the beach—"and then they came after me."

"When the shark grabbed me, I caught hold of his snout and pulled and twisted, and finally pried open its jaws and pulled my arm out," he said. The bite "was like someone driving nails into my arm," Fryling added. "If that shark had sunk his jaws a little deeper into my arm it would have been the end of me."

Fryling was treated for eight puncture

wounds at Malibu Emergency Hospital; no stitches were required.

Fryling said the sharks averaged 2½ to 5 feet in length.

In the spring of 1960, 16-year-old Suzanne Theroit went on the annual picnic of the sophomore class of Mora Catholic High School, Watsonville, California.

Once at Hidden Beach, about six miles from Santa Cruz, California, Miss Theroit went in swimming. While holding onto an inner tube about 50 feet off shore, inside the breakers, she was struck by a shark. Nick Buak, 16, and Ray Cronin, 15, who were with her, said the shark, its dorsal fin about a foot out of the water, made one slashing grab at her and ripped the lower part of her left leg.

Screaming with pain and asking for a priest, Miss Theroit was pulled ashore by Cronin and Buak. A student applied a tourniquet, and she was rushed to the hospital. The leg had to be amputated above the knee.

The International Shark Attack File shows 46 attacks in California.

FLORIDA

On September 21, 1931, Miss Gertrude Holaday was swimming about 200 feet off the municipal beach at West Palm Beach, Florida. She had turned to head back to shore when she looked down and saw "a huge fish." She noticed that the water was red with blood. She had already been bitten on the thigh and calf. She screamed for help and pushed at the shark, meanwhile splashing as loudly and as strongly as she could.

Sam Barrows, the lifeguard on duty, seized a can buoy (with a lifeline) and swam out to her. He saw that the fish was an 8-foot hammerhead. Miss Holaday swam to him, leaving behind a trail of blood, while Barrows splashed to make the shark draw back. Barrows caught her hand and helped her hold on to the buoy. As they swam back to shore, Miss Holaday supported by the buoy on one side and by Barrows on the other. The hammerhead followed in so close that it could be seen by those on shore.

Miss Holaday had suffered several bites on

the right leg, and her left leg was lacerated—probably by contact with the shark's skin. She not only survived, but regained full use of both legs.

Longboat Key is south of Sarasota on Florida's west coast. There, on July 27, 1958, 8-year-old Douglas Lawton was ducking for shells with his 12-year-old brother, Robert, in two and a half feet of murky water, a few feet off shore. Their parents and aunt and uncle had just left the water when the shark attacked. It sank its teeth in Douglas's left thigh. Douglas screamed; Robert grabbed him and yelled for help. Trying to pull the shark off his brother, Robert was knocked around by its tail. The shark let go, but again locked its jaw into the thigh. Mr. Lawton and Douglas' uncle, raced into the water, and took hold of the boy and the shark. They managed to get Douglas up onto the beach. There Mr. Lawton applied a tourniquet and rushed Douglas to the hospital. The leg was amputated; Douglas Lawton survived.

The International Shark Attack File shows 107 attacks in Florida [including 17 in the Florida Keys.]

THE UNITED STATES

SOUTH CAROLINA

On May 29, 1919, Mr. W. E. Davis, went swimming in James Island Sound, near Charleston, S.C.

"On this particular afternoon, the tide was extremely high, even for a spring tide. So high, in fact, that it lacked less than an inch of covering the bridge. It was a perfectly calm afternoon with barely a ripple on the water. Following my custom I dove from the wharf and headed out into the sound. I had swum probably thirty yards when my left foot was seized. . . . I was conscious of no pain, only pressure. My instant and involuntary reaction was to jerk practically clear of the water, and due to the sharpness of the teeth holding me I succeeded in ripping my foot clear. I immediately turned around and headed for the bridge. As I did so I saw directly in front a swirling of the water and at the same time the white of a shark's stomach and the tip of its tail. Unthinkingly, in my haste to regain the wharf, I swam directly over this spot and in so doing experienced a sharp burning contact with some rough-skinned body. Fortunately I reached the wharf very shortly. I was pretty well knocked out but did notice that my foot was practically mangled from about five inches up the leg down. Also a raw spot where the rough skin had touched me. The lacerations on my foot continued out in cleanly defined cuts to the tips of my toes, indicating that the shark had really held on to the last.

". . . It must have been a vicious fish and an intentional attack because I had no warning whatsoever. Further, the water that afternoon was exceptionally clear so that the shark could not have been mistaken as to what it was attacking. Also I was swimming vigorously and making quite a commotion in the water. Under the conditions I think it was a hungry, vicious shark that intentionally attacked me, and had I been further out in the sound would have attacked me again."

When Mr. Davis was taken to the St. Francis Xavier Hospital in Charleston, it was at first thought that his foot would have to be amputated. Fortunately, this did not have to be done, and Mr. Davis regained the full use of it, although it required 70 odd stitches to close the lacerations.

Mr. Lewis Kornahrens was attacked while in the surf at Folly Island, S.C., on July 31, 1924. According to his chart in the Roper Hospital, where he was admitted the day the attack occurred:

"The patient says he was standing in the breakers near the seashore in water about waist deep. This was at Folly Beach near the Elks Club. He says something that he thinks was a fish grabbed on both legs at the same time and that he hit the fish (?) with his fist, whereupon it turned him loose. A man came to his assistance and helped him to shore. The patient says the man saw about six feet of the fish but didn't stop to observe closely." (signed) Dr. J. N. Walsh.

Mr. Kornahrens was treated for "repair of lacerated muscles on the left knee and leg," which required more than 100 stitches, and was discharged on August 28, 1924. Mr. Kornahrens continued to feel a severe pain in his knee cap and it grew steadily worse. Finally he was readmitted to the hospital on November 4, 1924. A minor operation was performed and a fragment of a tooth was taken from the vicinity of the knee cap. It was sent on for identification to the American Museum of Natural History of New York: "I am returning under separate cover today the tooth fragment you sent. This is not a barracuda tooth. There is no doubt on this point. Mr. Nichols and I are both satisfied that it is a fragment of a shark's tooth, and we are inclined to think that it is from one of the mackerel sharks, but presumably a young specimen."

On August 28, 1933, young Kenneth Layton and a friend were in bathing at Pawley's Island, S.C., which is about seventy-five miles north of Charleston, when they were startled by a cry of "Shark! Shark!" from a man standing on the beach.

At the place where they were bathing, the beach is very flat; consequently, they were well out from shore, although in water not much over four feet. Both he and his friend were terribly startled when they heard the cry of warning. Looking down the beach, they saw a large dorsal fin of a shark 50 yards away. They immediately rushed for shore. Layton says the shark deliberately tried to cut them off. When they reached water about waist deep, Layton was seized by the right heel and ankle. He struggled frantically, and in the meanwhile his friends who were bathing nearby were rushing to his assistance.

During his struggle and the commotion caused by the approach of his friends, the shark relinquished its hold.

Several tendons in Layton's leg, including the Achilles, had been severed, but he eventually recovered the full use of his foot.

On June 21, 1933, 15-year-old Drayton Hastie, of Charleston, S.C., was bathing at the north end of Morris Island, which is situated at the mouth of Charleston Harbor.

"... Far up the shore line I saw what I thought might be the dorsal fin of a large shark cutting the rough surface. I stood up and strained my eyes to make certain. Yes, it must be a fin, I concluded. ... Reaching the place and finding nothing that resembled a fin, I believed that I had mistaken a choppy wave for a fin. I did not like the idea of swimming with sharks all around, so I sat down in about three feet of water, at which place the beach sloped gradually until about six feet beyond where I was sitting, at the point, it made a deep drop. I was almost certain that in such swallow water I would be safe from anything large enough to bite.

"... I felt a swerve of water, which was immediately followed by an impact which

47

brought me to my senses. Something clamped down on my right leg. I was aware of a tearing pain up and down my leg, and that I was being pulled outward by something which seemed to have the power of a horse. Looking down, I saw, amid the foam and splashing, the head of a large shark with my knee in its mouth, shaking it as a puppy would shake a stick in attempting to take it away from some one. Through natural instinct, I started kicking frantically with my unharmed leg in order to free myself. I freed my right leg, only to have the monster bite me on my left one. All this time I had been pulling myself up on the beach backwards with my hands and kicking at the rough head of the shark, which seemed to me as solid as Gibraltar.

"... Although to you this may seem long and strung out, it must have all happened in a space of two seconds.

"... Although some people said I had been bitten by everything from crabs up to whales, I still have a perfect design of a shark's mouth around my knee, measuring ten inches across. This confirms the statement of my friend who was standing on the bank and who said that the shark was easily eight feet long."

Mr. Hastie, with much difficulty, was carried to the army hospital at Fort Moultrie, where first aid was administered. It required more than 30 stitches to close his wounds. Later he was transferred to Riverside Infirmary, in Charleston, where he remained a patient for two weeks.

Both the week before and the week after the attack on Mr. Hastie, two eight-foot sharks were taken within one hundred yards from where he had bathed. On identification they were found to be the yellow or cub shark (*Hypoprion brevirostris*), thought to be more a native of the West Indies than of the Atlantic Coast. The only previous record of this shark off Charleston was one small one taken on May 1882, and another small one taken in October, 1932.

On January 24, 1940, William M. Tanner was standing in the Atlantic Ocean at Folly Beach, S.C., in water three feet deep with swells three feet high. He was about two hundred and twenty-five feet from shore. Suddenly his ankle was seized by a shark. He braced his other foot in the sand and repeatedly beat the shark with his fists. Harvey H. Haley, who was six feet from Tanner, had been struck by the shark just before it attacked Tanner; and he lunged to Tanner, got hold of his wrist, and pulled backward to prevent Tanner's being taken into deeper water. He felt the shark under Tanner and kicked at it. The shark released its hold and did not attack again. Haley then aided Tanner, who hobbled on one foot, to wade to shore. Tanner's foot was badly mangled, but he recovered.

The kind of shark is unknown.

Haley was awarded a bronze medal by the Carnegie Hero Fund Commission for his assistance to Tanner.

In August, 1941, Howard E. Sweatmon, 20 years old, was swimming in chest-deep surf at Sullivan's Island, South Carolina when a shark surfaced, rolled over, and bit him on the chest. He struck at the shark with his fists, and the fish departed. Residents had sighted three large sharks in the vicinity previously.

At Little River Beach, South Carolina, in early July 1960, Dan Winsett and Ray Allen, both businessmen, and Monty Gray, a farmer, all from Dillon, South Carolina, were fishing. Winsett was fishing on the beach while Allen was in the surf. Gray was fishing on a sandbar a hundred yards out. Gray related:

"I saw Dan hook a big one. I pulled my gear in and went into the water. Suddenly I realized the big one was a six-foot shark. He snapped Dan's [40-pound test] line and lunged at me. He slashed into my left leg and hung on like a giant tick. I felt myself being pulled under. He was shaking me and pulling me out to sea at the same time.

"I had Ray's knife with me. I succeeded in partially clinching with the shark. At this point I managed to stab him near one of his fins. I managed to squash a thumb into a corner of the mouth. It was then that I said a little prayer. I figure the prayer worked. Suddenly I was free."

"That shark shook Monty like a dog shakes a chicken," Winsett said.

Gray's wrist was slashed and his calf required two hours of surgery.

The International Shark Attack File shows 23 attacks in South Carolina.

NORTH CAROLINA

Although not an attack on a human being, the following account of an encounter with tiger sharks in Beaufort Harbor, North Carolina, just south of Cape Lookout, gives food for thought. It is given here as reported by E. W. Gudger in the *Journal of the Mitchell Society* (1948).

"In 1914 the U.S. Fisheries steamer *Fish Hawk* was anchored off Fort Macon and near the inner mouth of Beaufort Inlet. Here she was surrounded by a small school of large tiger sharks. They were evidently ravenously hungry, for they swam around the vessel, apparently waiting for anything edible that might be thrown overboard, and they showed no fear of the men moving about but a few feet above them.

"A baited shark hook thrown overboard was seized by the largest (and presumably the leader) of the school, who departed "taking bait and hook with him." The next hook was snapped up by another shark, which was brought aboard and killed. The rebaited hook had no sooner reached the water than it was taken by a 10-ft., 1-in. tiger. It was killed and hung up by the tail from the end of the boom with the head clear of the water. What then took place was vividly described by [Lewis] Radcliffe as follows:

" 'About this time a shark, larger than any of those taken, swam up to the one hanging [by the tail] from the boom, and raising its head partly out of water, seized the dead shark by the throat. As it did so, the captain of the *Fish Hawk*, began shooting at it with a 32-caliber revolver. . . . The shots seemed only to infuriate the shark, and it shook the dead one so viciously as to make it seem doubtful whether the boom would stand the onslaught. Finally it tore a very large section of the unfortunate's belly, tearing out and devouring the whole liver, leaving a gaping hole across the entire width of the whole body large enough to permit a small child to easily enter the body cavity. At this instant, one of the bullets struck a vital spot, and after a lively struggle on the part of the launch's crew, a rope was secured around its tail.'

"These four tiger sharks, all females, were brought to the laboratory and measured. The largest was 12 ft. and its victim 10 ft., 1 in. long."

Gudger concluded: "there is every probability" that other tiger sharks "have entered the harbor. But if so they do not seem to have been seen, caught, or recorded."

The International Shark Attack File shows 2 attacks in North Carolina.

NEW JERSEY

In 1916 five shark attacks took place on the New Jersey shore in the space of ten days.

The first attack occurred at Beach Haven on July 2. Charles Van Zant, in swimming off the beach, was struck by a shark. Whether one leg or both were savaged is unclear from the contemporary accounts. He died as a result of the attack.

On July 6, at Spring Lake, about forty miles up the coast, Charles Pruder was in swimming. A shark pulled him under, and his blood stained the water's surface. Lifeguards got to Pruder by boat while he was still conscious, but death came fast. His right leg had been bitten off half way between ankle and knee, and his left foot was gone, and a bite had been taken out of his abdomen.

Then, on July 12, a shark struck in Matawan Creek, about 20 miles from Spring Lake. The creek is ten miles distant from the sea through Raritan Bay. It is 17 feet deep at its deepest, and nowhere more than 35 feet wide. Off the bank of the Matawan, twelve-year-old

Lester Stillwell went in swimming and disappeared beneath the surface. The shark had been seen. However, according to the *New York Times*, 24-year-old Stanley Fisher did not believe that a shark was responsible; he thought Lester had had a "fit." He entered the water; he came out with his right leg torn to the bone from the knee to the groin. Fisher died in the hospital; however, he stated that he had actually reached Lester's body and torn it away from the shark. The estimate of the shark's length was 10 feet.

Meanwhile, J. D. Dunn, a youth, was swimming half a mile downstream. There, as he pulled himself clear of the water, a shark tore the flesh of his left leg. He splashed with his right foot, and his friends pulled to help him; the shark let go. From the tooth marks, this shark's mouth was estimated to be 14 inches wide. Its length was estimated at nine feet.

On July 15, a 7½-foot "blue" shark was caught off Sea Bright, N.J. It contained human bone. It may have been the villain of the New Jersey attacks. However, another shark caught on July 17 also contained human remains.

That summer there were more and larger sharks than usual around New Jersey. The water temperature was higher than usual, and schools of sharks, many of unusual size (8-10 feet) had been reported heading north of Cape Hatteras and sighted off New York Harbor. That month large schools were also reported south of the Grand Banks.

It was suggested that the Gulf Stream might have been deflected nearer to the coast by cyclones, bringing the sharks with them; one observer also suggested that the near absence of shipping due to World War I had deprived Atlantic sharks of their usual garbage "handouts," thus increasing their hunger. On the other hand, another observer suggested that the attacks should be attributed to an increased appetite among sharks for human flesh due to wartime naval disasters.

The New York–New Jersey area was, of course, suddenly shark conscious and bounties on sharks were set in New Jersey. The concern even reached the national level; the House of Representatives voted $5,000 for the search for the New Jersey maneater.

One of the most surprising aspects of the Matawan Creek attacks was the distance from the open sea. Elsewhere in the book are accounts of well-documented shark attacks at Ahwaz, Iran, which is 90 miles upriver from sea. It may also be of interest to note that sharks live in Lake Nicaragua, a fresh-water body, and in 1944 there was a bounty offered for dead freshwater sharks, as they had "killed and severely injured lake bathers recently." These sharks grow to more than four feet in length. The position of the fins shows some variation from those of their Atlantic relatives.

But let us return to New Jersey. Between 1916 and 1960 only nine attacks took place on the New Jersey shore. Then, on August 21, 1960, 24-year-old John Brodeur and his fiancee, Jean Filoramo, were standing in waist-deep, somewhat murky water at about 3:30 in the afternoon. Brodeur was about 75 feet from the shore at Sea Girt, New Jersey, and he was waiting for a wave to ride in. As one wave went by, "I saw a long blackish object about ten yards away, sticking out of the wave and being carried toward shore."

Brodeur dismissed it as "probably a man," and turned back toward the open sea, looking for the right wave. "Something hit me from behind, and I felt a tremendous jerking pull on my right leg." He slapped the water, kicked "something rough" with his left foot, and hit it with his hand. Seeing the water turn red with blood, he yelled to his fiancee. She rushed to him and, holding him up, yelled for help. Three men, including Miss Filoramo's father, came out to them and helped them ashore.

Brodeur's leg was amputated at the knee.

At the end of the same month, at Ocean City, New Jersey, about seventy miles south, Richard Chung, a medical student, was bitten and later underwent surgery.

It was again a summer of unusual shark catches, as in 1916. Fishermen reported that they were finding "five and six times" as many sharks as usual in pound nets.

The International Shark Attack File shows 17 attacks in New Jersey.

"I didn't stay to watch him. I hollered

RHODE ISLAND

This undated newspaper account decribes an encounter with a shark by a skindiver:

"Howard LaPorte, 19, a state life guard and former all-state hockey star at Burrillville High School, escaped unharmed after fighting off a shark, 15 feet under water at East Matunuck, R.I.

"LaPorte, pale and shaken, and a spear-fishing companion, Clark A. Sammartino, 23, of Providence, swam ashore near Deep Hole, scene of the encounter.

" 'We were going for stripers,' he said. 'Clark was about 20 yards on the sea side of me. I had a funny feeling something was behind me. As I turned I saw the shark coming for me. He was shiny, moving fast. He was on his side with his mouth open.

" 'I just had time to fire the spear. It caught him just inside the corner of his mouth. It happened very fast. He turned and flicked his tail. It knocked the gun from my hand. Then he took the spear and swam away.

" 'I didn't stay to watch him. I hollered to Clark, then headed for shore. I bet I set the Olympic record for 30 yards.' "

The International Shark Attack File shows no attacks in Rhode Island.

MASSACHUSETTS

While swimming in water twenty feet deep in Buzzards Bay, at Mattapoisett, Massachusetts, on July 25, 1936, Joseph C. Troy, Jr. was carried under the surface by a shark at a point three hundred and fifty feet from shore. Walter Norris Stiles, doing a quiet sidestroke, was swimming within six feet of Joseph, who was using the noisier "crawl." Calling "Shark, bring your boat" to a man in a sailboat moored a hundred and fifty feet farther from shore, Stiles trod water and looked over the water for sharks, his understanding being that they swam in pairs. Within twenty seconds Joseph rose, his leg having been bitten from the hip to the knee; but Stiles did not know of this injury. Stiles swam a stroke or two to him, noted he had an expression of agony, and asked him whether he could put his hands on Stiles' shoulders. Joseph simply said "No." Stiles then locked his arm in Joseph's, yelled again to the man, and swam toward the boat. In the meantime the man had entered the tender of his boat, and he rowed to Stiles and Joseph, reaching them in two minutes. Stiles

took hold of the boat, and the man pulled
Joseph into it. Stiles climbed in without aid.
About that time a shark appeared headed
toward the side of the boat but swerved and
disappeared beneath the surface at a point
three feet from the boat. The man rowed to
shore. Joseph lapsed into unconsciousness and
was removed to a hospital. Three hours later,
while his leg was being amputated, he died.
Joseph had lost a finger and had many lacerations on both hands (presumably from hitting the shark), as well as his left thigh torn
to ribbons.

Stiles was awarded a bronze medal by the
Carnegie Hero Fund Commission.

Dr. Hugh M. Smith, formerly head of the
United States Fisheries Bureau, who had a
summer home at Woods Hole on Buzzards
Bay, expressed the opinion that the shark in
this case was a maneater (*Carcharodon carcharias*). Smith was reported by the *New
York Times* as having records of twenty defi-
nite sightings of the great white in and near
Buzzard's Bay over the previous fifty years,
the most recent having been in 1927.

The International Shark Attack File shows 4
attacks in Massachusetts.

OTHER STATES

The International Shark Attack File shows attacks in other states as follows:

Connecticut	1
Delaware	2
Georgia	6
Mississippi	1
New York	8
Texas	6
Virginia	2

ELSEWHERE
IN
THE
AMERICAS

MONA ISLAND, P.R.

On Saturday, July 5, 1952, Señor Juan Suarez-Morales, then Librarian of the University of Puerto Rico at Mayaguez, decided to go spear fishing off Mona Island, which lies some fifty miles east of Puerto Rico. On this particular morning, the land temperature was about 88°F and the crystal-clear water was relatively warm.

Wearing a yellow bathing suit, a white polo shirt, blue fins, mask and snorkel, and armed with a spear fishing gun, Señor Morales entered the sea at about 7:30 a.m. For the first hour and a half, he poked around an area of reefs and shoals black with a multitude of small fish which had already attracted schools of several species of larger fish. His first shot got him a large shad which he carried to the beach. He then returned to the shoals to resume his sport.

At this time, approximately 9:00 a.m., Morales became aware of the presence of a shark which apparently had followed him towards the shore, probably attracted by the struggles of the speared shad. The shark, estimated by the hunter to be about five feet long, had clean-swept lines and was colored dark above and white below. However, it gave him no concern and he shooed it away with a wave of his spear.

Continuing his fishing, Morales missed his second shot and was forced to dive to recover his spear. At this time, about ten minutes after his first kill, "I had the sensation that there was something behind me," wrote Morales. "And indeed, it was 'el Señor Tiburon' ready to leap forward." But, with a rapid movement of his spear gun, Morales frightened the shark away. He went on fishing, albeit with growing caution, spearing a five-pound mackerel, which he fastened to his belt. During this interval, the shark was seen repeatedly in the offing until about 10:00 a.m., when it disappeared. Shortly thereafter, Morales' spear head became loosened and he decided to return to the dock a distance across the water of about one hundred and fifty yards. Because of the weight of his catch, now tied to the useless spear gun, and the awkwardness of walking with fins, he decided to swim back, parallel to the shore.

"At the start, I again encountered the

shark. I recall that I was worried by such an assiduous body guard and having no other weapon, I threw a couple of stones at him to chase him away. I decided to walk a little in order to fool the shark. After walking a good stretch, I threw myself into the sea and swam about 30 feet from shore in water between 10 to 12 feet deep. Once, the fish came loose and floated on the water several feet away. I went after them and secured them better. From time to time and in between small rests, I could already see the dock. A few minutes more and the task would be ended." It was now almost 11:00 a.m.

"In this area, there are rocks near the shore so I had to swim out somewhat. I was pushing the fish ahead of me as I swam. Then, without warning, I felt as if I had been struck by a rocket or as if an animal was repeatedly jumping on me. It was the shark which, coming up from behind, had seized me by the knee. I felt no pain, no fear, no panic." There was no time to call for help because the shark's lunge pulled Morales violently to the bottom.

"I was wearing mask and snorkel which helped me a great deal since I could actually see my enemy and fight him the best I could without swallowing too much water. I released my load and tried to fight the shark by punching him on the nose with my fist, but the animal would not let go . . . Then came to me—like a flash—the idea of pushing in the eyes of my enemy . . . As soon as I pressed down on those far-apart, hard eyes, the shark let go, disappearing in the cloud of blood. I made land in no time." And by shouting in English, then Spanish, Morales succeeded in attracting help.

"The wound was deep and lacerated with a bone fracture on the right side below the knee." Morales estimated that the attack lasted about 60 seconds. At this time, "when the shark seized, I sort of laughed to myself on the futility of life . . . I thought that if the shark snapped off my leg, I should get rid of my mask and snorkel and swallow water to avoid a slow and painful death . . ." After reaching shore, Morales said, he tried to walk but could not, adding: "I don't think I was scared to the point of shock . . ." While being ferried to the dock, Morales asked the boatman to go by the place of attack to see if he could recover his spear gun and fish. The man refused—"obstinately."

THE BAHAMAS

John Fenton went diving 40 feet down in the Middle Bight, Andros Island, in the Bahamas. He was testing an underwater camera, and was wearing a diving suit. A nurse shark, which is generally described as harmless, appeared. Fenton patted it on the head; it lashed out at his arm, catching only the sleeve of the diving suit. Fenton killed it with his knife. Even after death the grip was not released. Fenton had to cut the sleeve off. Fenton reported that it twisted and shook like a bulldog. The shark proved to be 7 feet, 7 inches long. When the incident was reported in *Popular Science*, Fenton remarked that "it looked twice as big."

GULF OF PANAMA

Reported by Capt. B. H. Kean of the U.S. Army Medical Corps.

On September 23, 1943, in a shallow cove about 75 feet off the north shore of Rey Island, Gulf of Panama, Pacific Ocean, a Navy boat had anchored. No refuse had been dumped into the cove, and no sharks were seen.

At 2:35 p.m., a sailor aged 20, wearing swimming trunks, dived into the water to determine if the ship's propeller had been fouled or damaged. As he came up he was attacked by a "maneater" shark 6 or 7 feet long which was seen at close range by the captain and by several members of the crew. It was impossible to shoot the fish without subjecting the sailor to danger, for both were thrashing about, the shark making repeated attacks. The injured man was lifted on deck within one minute of the initial attack. A tourniquet was applied to the left thigh, emergency dressings were appropriately placed, and he was rushed to the local Naval hospital, where he arrived three hours later, exsanguinated and in shock.

Following the administration of anti-shock measures, he was taken to the operating room where the left popliteal artery was repaired, the popliteal vein was ligated and muscle groups were rapidly approximated. A tip of a tooth found beneath the muscles in the popliteal fossa was removed. The patient died in shock four hours after admission and seven hours after the initial injuries were received.

A complete autopsy, including examination of the head, was performed at the Board of Health Laboratory, Gorgas Hospital, 11 hours after death. A tooth pattern suggestive of two, three and four rows of teeth could be recognized in several of the series or sets of lacerations.

Set A, which consisted of twelve individual lacerations averaging 15 cm. in length, arranged in two rows, extended deeply into the left knee joint. The medial condyle of the femur, especially the cartilaginous surface, was crushed. Wedged into niches in the condyle were fragments of teeth, the largest measuring 1 cm. in its greatest dimension.

Several other tiny, irregular fragments of teeth were found in the periosteal tissue.

The tips of two teeth, one removed from the popliteal fossa by surgeon and one removed from the medial condyle of the left femur, were shown to Mr. John T. Nichols, curator of recent fishes, of the American Museum of Natural History, who identified them as "tips of the teeth of a small so-called maneater shark *Carcharodon carcharias*, and from a small individual of this species probably not more than 7 feet or so long."

In 1929 another attack in the same general area had been reported.

Abraham Moreno, 17, post office employee, Panama City, on November 4, 1928, was swimming with companions in Taboga Island Bay, about 35 miles from Rey Island. Moreno, clinging to their boat, left and started back for shore. Less than 50' from shore in about 6' of water, he was struck 3 to 4 times. He was pulled into the boat dead. One leg was gone, the second was amputated between the ankle and knee, the abdominal wall was gone and the intestines were protruding; his chest was wounded, 5 fingers gone, and there were three fractures in his right arm. A shark, caught within 2 hours, was found to contain a leg and part of a bathing suit. It was species *tintorera negra* or *jaba;* often found in those waters during the latter part of rainy season and not considered dangerous.

DEEP OCEAN:
THE
REPORTS
OF
MEN
ADRIFT
AT
SEA

When jets replaced propeller-driven aircraft on over-water flights, aircraft losses at sea declined sharply. This also dramatically reduced shark attacks in the open ocean. World War II and the postwar years saw a peaking in open-ocean shark attacks which brought to light the particular aggressiveness of white-finned sharks and the high mortality from their persistent attacks. Military and civilians suffered alike, as shown in *Airmen against the Sea* and in other open-ocean shark attack accounts in *Sharks and Survival*. Now the hazard is greatest along beaches, to bathers and snorkel divers, and to the more adventurous scuba divers fishing and exploring away from the crowds at popular oceanside resorts.

Loss of life at sea during World War II resulted in many tragic incidents to military personnel who were mentally and physically unprepared to cope with this survival problem. Since sharks were in the marine domain, the U. S. Navy took command of the problem. Their first effort was to seek advice from fish experts and other possible shark experts. The latter included a number of eminent scholars— like E. W. Gudger of the American Museum of Natural History, and F. A. Lucas and Charles William Beebe of the New York Zoological Society. Gudger refused to believe that men could be eaten by sharks; Lucas denied that sharks were a danger to man; and Beebe took the stand that sharks were no more to be feared than minnows. In the face of such pronouncements, lesser experts fell into line.

As a consequence, the Navy's approach was strictly academic. It issued a technical order that sharks were no great problem. This action was thought to be psychologically correct, but as events later showed the problem was merely swept under the rug. The psychological ploy was further expanded into a droll training manual, *Shark Sense*, with a total disregard for facts or reason. Maloney of *Colliers* rewrote it into a feature article—"The Shark Is a Sissy" —for civilian consumption. In the author's words, ". . . men who know sharks best, fear them least." It was, in Coppleson's words, so much baloney. Looking back, it seems more like a death warrant made out in the name of the reader.

Fortunately, Harold T. Coolidge, a zoologist on special duty to the White House, had access to secret reports on casualties and he initiated action for development of a shark deterrent. The first effort was a compilation of records, and foremost among these were V. M. Coppleson's 1933 records of Australian shark attacks. These and other documented records were copied from open scientific journals and stamped Top Secret.

In 1944, a product consisting of copper acetate and nigrosine—a dye—mixed with carbowax was distributed to the armed forces under the name "Shark Chaser." It failed miserably to live up to its name, but its usefulness as a shark repellant or deterrent was questioned for the first time in the analysis of 2500-survival accounts made by myself. My report appeared in the mid-1950's at a time when commercial airlines were weighing the advisability of providing shark repellent with life vests for passengers. It was an unfortunate timing. Manufacturers preparing to sell surplus supplies to commercial airlines were put out. Airline authorities were willing to deal with the issue, but with a minimum of publicity since it was bad for business. The Navy felt that its reputation was at stake. While it was generally agreed that the "Shark Chaser" might well be useless in a confrontation with a shark, it was highly regarded for its psychological value.

My meeting with Commander Clement Vaughn of the Air Search and Rescue Agency in 1952 had been a most fortuitous event. He turned over to me 2500-odd accounts of wartime survivors. These records were transferred to the Air Force Records Center at Maxwell Air Force Base, Alabama, where I was employed by the Arctic, Desert, Tropic Information center (ADTIC). All of the research was done in my leisure time, since ADTIC's interest was geared to land problems of survival, but when completed the analysis was issued under the stamp of the Air University. I was struck from the beginning by the small number—38—of accounts including actual contact with sharks; only 12 of these resulted in reported injuries or casualties. Gradually it dawned on me that if sharks were successful, there would be few records.

The following accounts are taken from my *Airmen against the Sea, An Analysis of Sea Survival Experiences*.

Here is the report of a Naval officer:

A Navy pilot who ditched off Kikai-Shima in the northern Ryukyus entered the water fully dressed except for his shoes, and was supported by a Mae West for the 1¼ hours he remained in the water before rescue:

"Fifteen minutes after landing, W. discovered a shark about 6 feet long, 5 to 6 feet below the water and directly under him. The shark made no runs at him and W. took no affirmative action except to swim easily which was all that was necessary in order to stay up in the water ... A second shark about 10 to 12 feet long was not noted until the last 20 minutes before pickup. It might have been around during the whole period but W. did not see it until it was about 5 feet away and after it had come to the surface when the dorsal fin and tail projected above the water. At this time he used dye to indicate his position to the approaching plane, and while holding in the dye, the second shark swam through the discolored area with no indication that it saw W."

Another pilot swimming ashore in the Southwest Pacific had at least four sharks come within 25 yards of him, and not one of them made a determined attack. The amount of clothing he wore is not mentioned in his story:

"I left the raft at 1000 because I could see

the shore ... after a 2-hour swim I seemed to be a little closer ... a few minutes later while swimming on my back I looked to my left and about 3 feet away I saw a shark's fin and he was swimming along beside me. He then turned into me so I rolled over quickly and pushed him away with my right arm. He went out in front of me a few yards and did a 180-degree turn and came back under my stomach. I thrashed the water with arms and legs and I think I scared him away.... About 2 hours later there were two of them about 25 yards behind me, and seemed to be following me. After another hour of swimming I saw a splash and a shark's fin in front of me and about ten yards to my left.... I began to realize it was a swim for my life, so made up my mind not to get panicky but to keep plugging along until I got there, or the sharks got me."

A Navy ensign who parachuted into Philippine waters off Cape Engano during the carrier strike in October 1944 was just as lucky:

"D. hit the water on his back. He received quite a jolt but was able to untangle himself and get out of his shoes and back pack. He found his liferaft had shaken off when his parachute opened. The front half of his life jacket had a rip in it and the back half had to be inflated orally every half hour.... As he swam his socks gradually worked off, leaving his feet as a lure for sharks . . . which promptly put in an appearance. He was shadowed by about four sharks, 4 to 5 feet in length. They did not bother him as long as he continued to kick. As soon as he stopped to rest, one of them would make a pass at him. All of these were dry runs except one in which the shark grazed his legs and left tooth marks. He was picked up by a destroyer after 8 hours in the water."

A Naval officer spent 12 hours in the water off Guadalcanal after his destroyer was sunk. Wearing a kapok lifejacket, but without trousers, shoes, or socks, he supported himself through the night by hanging to two aluminum powder cans about 2 feet long and 5 inches in diameter. At dawn he was relaxed and floating in the water when he felt a scratching, tickling sensation in his left foot:

"Slightly startled, I ... held it up. It was gushing blood ... I peered into the water ... not 10 feet away was the glistening, brown back of a great fish ... swimming away. The real fear did not hit me until I saw him turn and head back toward me. He didn't rush ... but breaking the surface of the water came in a steady direct line. I kicked and splashed tremendously, and this time he veered off me ... went off about 20 feet and swam back and forth. Then he turned ... and came from the same angle toward my left ... When he was almost upon me I thrashed out ... brought my fist down on his nose ... again and again. He was thrust down about 2 feet ... swam off and waited. I discovered that he had torn off a piece of my left hand. Then ... again at the same angle to my left ... I managed to hit him on the eyes, the nose. The flesh was torn from my left arm ... At intervals of ten or fifteen minutes he would ease off from his slow swimming and bear directly toward me, coming in at my left. Only twice did he go beneath me. Helpless against this type of attack I feared it most but because I was so nearly flat on top of the water, he seemed unable to get at me from below ... The big toe on my left foot was dangling. A piece of my right heel was gone. My left elbow, hand, and calf were torn. If he did not actually sink his teeth into me, his rough hide would scrape great pieces off my skin. The salt water stanched the flow of blood somewhat and I was not conscious of great pain." [In the excitement of trying to attract the attention of a ship going by, the officer forgot the shark, which struck again and bit into his thigh, exposing the bone. At this point he was seen, and several sailors with rifles on the ship began firing at the shark.] "A terrible fear of being shot to death in the water when rescue was so near swept over me. I screamed and pleaded and cried for them to stop. The shark was too close. They would hit me first."

Clothing and a pair of binoculars were apparently the decisive factors in the 16 hour survival of Lieutenant (j.g.) A. G. Reading, who had to ditch when the engine of his S2N failed 68 miles east of Wallis Island in the Central Pacific. He was knocked unconscious by the impact, but his radioman, E. H. Almond, managed to lift him from the cockpit, and put on and inflate his lifejacket for him before the plane sank. Here are the significant parts of Lieutenant Reading's report:

"After I came to, Almond told me the plane had sunk in 2 minutes and that he didn't have time to salvage the liferaft. He pulled both our 'dye markers' and had a parachute alongside of him. He did not have any pants on at all except for shorts. . . . We soon lost the chute and began drifting away from the dye. It was within a very short time (about ½ hour) when sharks were quite apparent swimming around us. A. and I were tied together by the dye marker cords and it made it difficult to make any headway. An hour later we heard aircraft and I said to Almond, 'Let's kick and splash around to see if we can't attract their attention.' It failed, but suddenly Almond said he felt something strike his right foot and that it hurt. I told him to get on my back and keep his right foot out of the water, but before he could, the sharks struck again and we were both jerked under water for a second. I knew that we were in for it as there were more than five sharks around and blood all around us. He showed me his leg and not only did he have bites all over his right leg, but his left thigh was badly mauled. He wasn't in any particular pain except every time they struck I knew it and felt the jerk. I finally grabbed my binoculars, and started swinging them at the passing sharks. It was a matter of seconds when they struck again. We both went under and this time I found myself separated from Almond. I also was the recipient of a wallop across the cheek bone by one of the flaying tails of a shark. From that moment on I watched Almond bob about from the attacks. His head was under water and his body jerked as the sharks struck it. As I drifted away . . . sharks continually swam about and every now and then I could feel one with my foot. At midnight I sighted a boat and was rescued after calling for help."

Then there was the 31-hour survival of an Ecuadorian flight officer who, with two companions, ditched off the coast of Ecuador on a flight between Esmereldas and Salinas. The three men removed their clothing before entering the water; all had life vests. One man was hurt and bleeding freely from the nose.

"All this occurred Thursday approximately between four and five of the afternoon. Then placing myself between them so that they could take hold of the harness of my life preserver we proceeded swimming. . . . Later night fell and the desperation and terrification of my companions was increasing progressively as the sea in that section is very rough and the waves caused my companions to swallow water as they had absolutely no control. It was there that my Colonel B., at a time estimated by me some five hours after the moment of the accident, died.

"Afterwards putting the corpse, which floated perfectly, in front of me I continued

pushing it, with the objective of taking it out
. . . if we managed to reach land. When I had
pushed the corpse of my Colonel ahead of me
in order to swim to it again, a strange force
dragged the body and I did not again see it in
spite of searching a long time among the
waves. Sub-Lieutenant D., who was still living, and who had hold of me, made me reflect
that it was foolish to wait longer and I continued toward where I believed the coast to be.
Sub-Lieutenant D. lived perhaps four or five
hours more until at the end, after having had
moments before his death of a state of despair
which is very painful to narrate, he died. Taking the same attitude as toward that of the
corpse of my Colonel, I put the body of my
companion in front of me and continued pushing him but not as far ahead as I had done
previously with the other corpse. As it was a
moonlight night, and during some moments
very clear, I was able to observe that strange
figures crossed very close to us, until at a
given moment I felt that they were trying to
take away the corpse pulling it by the feet, on
account of which I clutched desperately the
body of my companion and together with him
we slid until the tension disappeared. . . . Once
refloated, with despair I touched his legs and

became aware that a part of them was lacking
. . . and continued swimming with the now
mutilated corpse until the attack was repeated two times more and then, terrorized at
feeling the contact of fish against my body,
turned loose the corpse . . . convinced that I
would be the next victim until daybreak occurred. As soon as it was light I could see the
coast at a great distance but I had no hopes of
reaching it because with the light of day I
could clearly see that various sharks were following me. . . . When I moved my legs slowly,
with the object of resting, I touched with my
feet the bodies of these animals which were
constantly below mine in order to attack me.
I would then thrash the water and thus for a
few moments the danger would pass. I continued swimming all day Friday until at sundown I found myself some four or five
hundred meters from the rock on the coast,
and as I was already tired . . . because of the
undertow which existed I could not reach the
rocks until after making a superhuman effort
. . . at which hour I do not know . . ."

The longest shark survival incident occurred in the Pacific and lasted 42 hours.
Eight of the 12 men who survived the
ditching were fully clothed although some re-

moved or lost their shoes after entering the water. They held themselves up with a salvaged wing float and a sleeping bag, and in addition lashed themselves together. Later, they found a package of emergency food, a blanket, and a thermos half-filled with water. One of the survivors was located by the firing of his .45 automatic, and as he swam towards the group, his companions cautiously watched his approach for fear that he was out of his mind and might shoot them. One man died and his life vest was taken by another who had none. About this time, sharks appeared and the men tried to drive them away by shooting and kicking. Although they were not bothered particularly by sharks during darkness, they continued kicking. At daybreak, one man was bitten slightly, became frightened, and died during the second night. Two others became delirious and had to be protected because they made no effort to help themselves. At 0500 of the third morning, the remaining six men were rescued by a passing merchant vessel whose look-out reported sighting a rocket, although none was fired. The rescuers were greatly agitated by the presence of sharks among the survivors, one of whom noted it and remarked: "We got a kick out of it."

Almost all the reported casualties from shark attack were of men in the water, swimming or supported by a lifejacket, but there were exceptions, and men on liferafts were by no means immune to attack.

In practically all the raft narratives reviewed, the survivors had time enough to reach the safety of their platform before the sharks appeared. In 11 of the 38 accounts reporting the presence of sharks, the sharks appeared within 30 minutes after the men had taken to the water. In 36 accounts sharks appeared in the first 24 hours. In some accounts of long duration in tropic waters men reported their first and sometimes only shark on the 4th, 9th, or even 13th day.

Sharks were rarely noted until they came to the surface, usually some distance from the raft, "lazily cruising around." On approaching the raft, most sharks submerged and swam underwater before reappearing on the surface. In very few incidents did sharks approach the raft directly on the surface unless there was vomit or blood in the vicinity of the raft. In these instances, survivors remarked that the sharks appeared excited and "made passes at the raft."

"About 1000 I saw a large fin ... come toward the life raft along the streak of the dye marker. It disappeared some distance away, ... shortly afterward reappeared ... and swam directly toward the raft, approaching quite close, it submerged and swam directly under the raft ... it was about 12 feet long. It rolled over and reappeared on the other side ... we all sat very quiet, stopped bailing out the bloody vomit, and the radar man abandoned the idea of defecating over the side for fear of capsizing. The shark repeated this behavior several times at varied intervals but at no time seemed concerned with us or touched the raft."

In another case, this one off Japan in June, after the survivors had been vomiting into the water for about half an hour, eight sharks made passes at the raft as if to upset it. Although the men fired some 30 rounds of .38 caliber at them, it was another 1½ hours before the sharks left.

Sharks sometimes remained under the raft day and night, and often bumped against the raft bottom. Off Iwo Jima in early summer:

"The raft was followed a great part of the

time [10 days] by sharks ... frequently close enough to cause fear of upset ... On two occasions ... shot a shark from above ... each time, the shark sounded and did not bother them again. These fish came close enough so that they could almost be touched. Aside from the nuisance, they did not bother the raft."

The mere presence of sharks close by can be unnerving. They exerted enough force against the raft deck at times to lift the occupant 3 or 4 inches into the air; this was painful to those whose buttocks ached from raft drumming, and made sleep impossible.

One 17-day group of survivors stated that sharks never left them, and became increasingly bolder, leaping out of the water and spraying the occupants, or battering the soft deck fabric with their tails while trying to stun the fish under the raft:

"Late in the afternoon a shark about four feet long struck at the raft and going right over my shoulder slid into the raft. It took a bite out of C. One of the men and myself caught the shark by the tail and pulled him out of the raft. C. became delirious and died about four hours later ..."

Sharks habitually follow floating objects because the smaller fish on which they feed take refuge in the shadows. Several survivors commented that the sharks' interest in the raft was not for its occupants, but for the fish that clustered beneath it:

"I believe that it was feeding on the small fish in the shade of the raft. There might have been more than one shark. After the animal demonstrated its benign attitude toward us, our chief concern was that it would abrade our boat with its hide and deflate it, or that it would accidentally capsize us ... Its approach was heralded by panicked flights of flying fish. ... It was always chasing fish out into the open and feeding on them."

An F4U pilot who spent 9 days in a raft drifting from Rabaul to Bougainville wrote:

"From practically the first day, sharks were continually hitting up against the boat trying to get the small fish under it. I was quite scared at first, but soon got accustomed to it when I learned what they were after."

Recognition of this aspect of shark behavior gave the man in the raft some comfort and helped make the situation bearable, borne out by such remarks as "Sharks around all the time—no bother," and "he never came very close and did not constitute a problem." But though men sometimes achieved a sense of

SHARKS

Mako shark. Pacific makos are credited with 15 human attacks, Atlantic makos with two. (All figures refer to documented attacks listed in the International Shark Attack Files.)

Great white shark. Carcharodon Carcharias (white sharks) are credited with 22 human attacks.

Great white
attacking a bait of horsemeat.

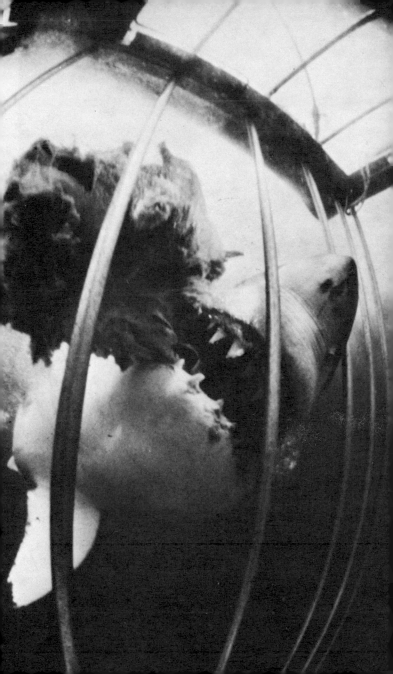

MARINELAND OF FLORIDA

Mako shark

Tiger shark
devouring a lemon shark (above).

PETER STACKPOLE, TIME, INC.

Tiger sharks (below)
are credited with 22 human attacks.

UPI

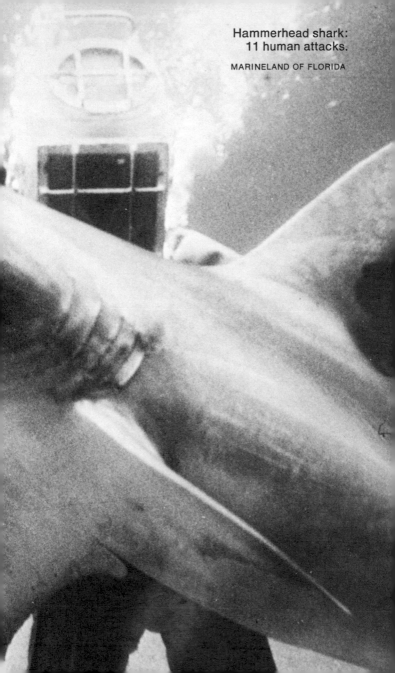

Hammerhead shark:
11 human attacks.

MARINELAND OF FLORIDA

Sand tiger sharks (Odontaspididae)

Tiger shark

UPI

Great white shark

Great white shark

NATIONAL AUDUBON SOCIETY

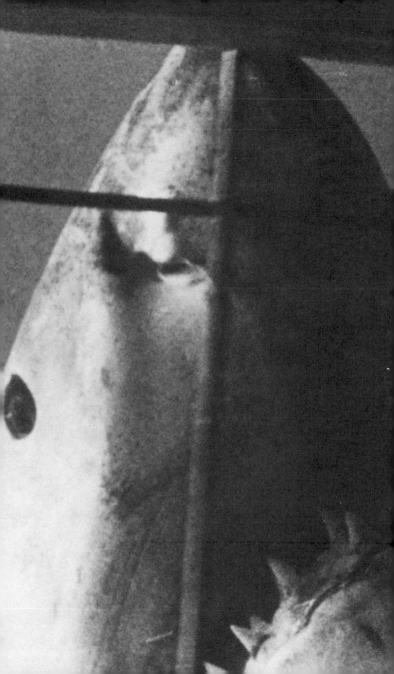

The teeth of a great white
MARINELAND OF FLORIDA

Blue shark: nine human attacks

UPI

Sand tigers

The fins of a hammerhead   BRUCE COLEMAN INC.

confidence toward sharks, situations developed which sorely tried their faith:

"He never came very close and did not constitute a problem until two unidentified planes appeared on the horizon at 1,000 feet and coming toward us. We were just debating which was worse, sharks or a strafing by Japs, when they veered off. A few hours later a submarine appeared, and again we debated whether to go overside with the shark or sweat it out in the raft."

"Half a dozen sharks were with me day and night. Only one, however made an attempt to attack, and it was a small one about 4 feet long. Most of them that I saw were at least 6 or 7 feet in length. My lone would-be attacker rolled over on its side and turned almost belly-up to get into position to bite. I could see its curved mouth, ugly teeth, and beady pig-like eyes ... fortunately he failed to carry out his attack."

Although a few men became accustomed to sharks around their raft, all raft occupants regarded them at least with suspicion if not with fear, and tried in one way or another to drive them away. All expressed relief at their departure.

Though most men remained quiet when a

large shark cruised nearby in hopes they would not be noticed, some tried to drive away smaller sharks circling around them by spanking the water with their paddles. In several of these cases the sharks were attracted to the paddles and tried to bite them. The interrogators usually interpreted this reaction as one of attack, but few of these incidents can be regarded as an unprovoked or deliberate attack on a liferaft by a shark.

Several incidents where men on rafts shot at sharks have already been mentioned. One of the most informative personal narratives in this regard is that of a Navy fighter pilot who was forced down in St. George's Channel between New Britain and New Ireland during the Rabaul strikes, and spent 8 days in his dinghy before being picked up by a Dumbo off Cape St. George. He was able to inflate and crawl into his raft a few minutes after ditching. He vaguely remembered something striking his foot while he was in the water. He then noticed he had lost the heel and part of the back of his left shoe, and from the scratches on the shoe hazarded a guess that a shark had bitten it off, though he saw no sharks at all until sundown of his third day when:

"There was a constant cloud of minnows following the boat at all times. I believe they fed on the minute marine life that collected on its bottom, sides, etc. That night larger fish came to feed on those minnows, then larger ones to get them; finally the boys with the peculiar dorsal fins arrived to see what the fuss was about. There were three of them that I could see.

"Finally one of them flashed directly under the boat hitting it with his back. He then turned and started striking it with his head. About the third time he came up to the boat slowly right on the surface and I shot him through the head from point-blank range. He thrashed for nearly a minute, then I could see him sinking down. The others did not touch him. One other shark still stayed about 10 feet away and I fired at his fin scaring him off. After it became dark I had no more trouble.

"That night [his 5th] I shot another shark and tried to bring him aboard, as I'd heard their liver, heart, etc. were good, but he was too slimy and still thrashing around slightly so I gave up. I also found that their hide was like 00 sandpaper!

"[At sundown on his 6th night] The usual ruckus of feeding fish started around the boat and shortly afterwards the sharks arrived. After swimming directly under the boat several times and hitting it with his back and fin, one large one, about seven feet (formerly the sharks had averaged about four to five feet) came to the surface and started to bump the boat with his nose.

"This had become a rather commonplace procedure with me by this time and I put the .45 about six inches from his head and was about to give him his iron for the day. The gun would not fire as the slide had rusted and wasn't all the way forward. Frantically I tried to push it home as the shark unmolested started banging my boat in earnest. Finally, in my excitement, I ejected the shell and it landed in the bottom of the boat and cleverly concealed itself under some other gear there. By now the shark was going berserk (evidently smelling me) and coming up underneath the boat and knocking us both completely out of the water. It then came to the surface again and made rushes at me, spinning the boat completely around 360 degrees several times.

"During all this I was holding grimly on and although I have no recollection of it, undoubtedly screaming! He came to the surface again, lay on his back, and began snapping at

the boat. Never was I so grateful to Mother
Nature for the placement of his mouth. I'd
given up trying to load the .45 and was swinging it by the muzzle at him. I smashed him in
the eye, on 'his very vulnerable nose', and his
'soft' belly. He turned over then and I started
to pound him on the top of the head. He was
as hard as steel there, and I later discovered
I'd partially flattened the little steel eyelet on
the butt of the gun where the lanyard is attached. He rolled over again still snapping at
the boat and I remembered a capsule of chlorine I had so I tried to get it out of my
pocket, with no success. I had dropped the
gun and was searching my pockets with one
hand and was hitting my voracious friend
with my other fist. In that ill-advised action, I
got two fair-sized splits in my forefinger, when
one of his snaps and one of my blows became
beautifully timed.

"Giving up the chlorine idea I seized the
dye marker can and dumped some of it in his
face, and the action ceased. The whole action
had lasted from five to ten minutes. Whether
the shark realized I was in the boat or
whether he was merely venting his rage on
this strange yellow object I will never know,
but he made a savage and sustained attack

and the ultimate end would have been the same, mine!

"After his departure I took stock of the situation and was depressed beyond all hope. The bottom of my boat had eighteen holes in it. One was a slit about four inches long, another a round hole about the size of my fist. The rest were assorted shapes and sizes, all smaller. This was not so bad, but at the small end of the boat in the inflated part there were five slits all leaking badly. I must confess I gave up and believing I was doomed, drank all my remaining water thinking that at least I didn't need to be thirsty any longer.

"[The 7th evening] My gun worked OK and I killed or badly wounded two sharks and had no further trouble. . . .

"After my first encounter with sharks, I never even considered going over the side of the boat to avoid strafing. . . . After the skirmishes with the sharks I'd have about five or ten small minnows in my boat and tried eating them. I thought they were better than the pemican."

AFRICA

SIERRA LEONE

This account, by James Boyle, of a savage shark attack and the victim's amazing recovery, was written in 1828.

On the 28th Sept. 1828, I was suddenly called to visit Thomas Corrigle, an apprentice on board the Britannia merchant-ship, (about 17 years old,) who, it was stated, was dreadfully mutilated by a shark whilst bathing up the river Sierra Leone, (twenty-five miles from Freetown), where the vessel was employed loading with timber.

On proceeding to examine the injured parts, I found that the left fore-arm had been removed within about two and a half inches of the elbow; the joint having been deeply penetrated by the animal's teeth, and the head of the ulna abruptly broken off from the body of the bone remaining attached.

The metacarpal bones of the right hand were denuded and fractured, whilst the ligamentous attachments of the wrist superiorly were all cut through, and both radius and ulna fractured at their lower extremities.

There was also a deep ragged wound in the palm of the hand, exposing the flexor tendons.

In the right groin there were two nearly parallel wounds, one about three, the other about two and one-half inches long, the latter dividing the skin and cellular substance, and bringing into view the lower portion of the tendon of the obliquis externus muscle.

The greater part of the testicle of the same side was exposed by an extensive division and a partial removal of its scrotal covering.

The right thigh, which afforded the most appalling spectacle I had ever seen before in the form of a wound, had yet to be closely examined. In the attack on this extremity the shark's teeth came in contact with the abdomen, about four inches internally. . . . From this, no doubt on account of its elasticity, the teeth glided down to the hip-joint. . . . Here the . . . animal succeeded in penetrating to the neck of the femur externally; thence he conducted a frightful wound downwards till within about four inches of the external condyle, where its course abruptly changed, crossing the thigh, and completely dividing the rectus femoris.

In the whole of this continuous track the femur was laid bare; all the fleshy mass covering the outside of the extremity admitting of such elevation, that it might have been easily removed by one sweep of the amputating knife.

Internally, a little behind the condyle,... [another] wound, continuing to the extent of about three and a half inches upwards, exposed the femoral artery.

It was for a moment a question how to dispose of so many alarming wounds then exhibited: the state of the thigh, particularly in a hot climate, appeared to call for amputation at the hip-joint; but the absolute necessity of removing both arms, in addition to the consideration of a probably extensive loss of blood previously to the patient's getting out of the water, rendered the prospect of success so faint as to be despaired of; it was, therefore, determined on to amputate both arms, which was accordingly immediately done—the left above the elbow, the right above the wrist— and to bring the divided fleshy mass of the thigh as nearly in apposition as its excessively lacerated condition would admit of. To accomplish the latter, 18 stitches by means of curved needles were made in the thigh alone.... and completing the dressing by sticking plaister, soft, simple dressing, and 18-

tailed bandage. All this the heroic boy bore without murmur. . . .

"[On October 2nd] the boy was entirely free from fever, and from this time not one unpleasant symptom took place. . . . The spirited youth, in robust health, and *without lameness*, quitted Sierra Leone for England on the 25th December, taking passage in the Champion timber-ship.

NATAL, SOUTH AFRICA

A series of shark attacks that brought with it an extraordinary mixture of human reactions occurred on the south coast of Natal, South Africa, in 1957–1958. The coast is accustomed to sharks, and over 30 attacks since World War II were on record. But the series of attacks that were to occur were outside Natal's experience.

The first victim, sixteen-year-old Bob Wherley, lost a leg to a shark on December 18, at Karridene, one of a string of resort towns closely spaced along the coast. On December 20, the second victim, Allan Green, who was fourteen, was attacked and killed at Uvongo Beach, roughly thirty miles south of Karridene.

The third, Vernon James Berry, arrived in Margate, only a few miles from Uvongo, for his holiday on December 23. That afternoon he went swimming. C. J. van der Merwe described what happened then:

"About 150 people were bathing in the sea, and a group of us, including Mr. Berry, were on the outer fringe in waist-deep water. It was about 4:30 p.m.

"We were only 30 yards from the shore when I saw a black fin in the waves less than 15 feet from me. I paid little attention to it because some of the bathers were wearing skin-diver's fins on their feet and I thought it was one of them playing in the waves.

"Suddenly the fin appeared again as it passed me and I was horrified to see that it was a monstrous shark more than 10 feet long. I shouted 'Shark! Shark!' to warn the other bathers. Just as I turned to leave the surf the monster attacked Mr. Berry a few paces away.

"He was floating when the first attack came. It was too horrible to watch as the shark tore at him with its huge jaws while he tried to fight it off with his bare hands.

"Again it came at him and he struggled free, his arm torn to ribbons right to the bone. Again the shark attacked with vicious bites, tearing the flesh from the man's side and thigh and shaking him like a cat does a mouse.

"While some men were dashing through the surf to help him a wave broke over man and shark and they parted. The shark then disappeared."

Berry died in the ambulance on the way to the hospital.

Despite the attack on December 23, over 100 people were swimming at Margate at noon on December 30. At an emergency meeting that morning the town had decided to build a lookout tower. Meanwhile, the council had hired a "shark spotter plane", which was circling over the beach. The sea was clear and calm.

Fifteen-year-old Julia Painting was about 30 yards from shore, in knee-deep water, a few paces from a large crowd. A "large" shark came in to attack. Paul Brokensha went to her aid. He punched at the shark as it tore at her—"like punching leather", he said—was knocked away by the shark's tail, but returned to the battle until the shark finally departed.

Julia lost her left arm, was savaged about the breast and buttocks, and was severely lacerated on the right hand by her attempts to beat the shark off. "Let me die, let me die, I am finished," she said on the beach. She survived, however, and would be able to leave the hospital by January 17.

The local authorities ordered nylon shark nets for the Margate beaches, and banned swimming until they were in place. They met to request aid from the South African government for setting up nets all along the Natal coast.

The South African Naval vessel *Vrystaat* was already en route to sink depth charges as a shark-killing measure. A suggestion that sharks be baited with balls of lard containing carbide—which forms a gas inside the shark causing it to float to the surface—ran into objections from the S.P.C.A. as being "unnecessarily cruel."

The plan to sink depth charges brought strong objections from Professor J.L.B. Smith, the icthyologist consulted, who pointed out that the many fish killed by depth charges would in fact draw sharks as to a feast. A fishing expert remarked, "It is the most stupid move imaginable." The Mayor of Durban—a resort at the northern end of the string of towns—which had restricted swimming to enclosed areas since before 1916—agreed.

Nevertheless, on January 6, the depth charging was begun. The officials felt that no harm would be done if sharks were attracted, since bathing was banned in any case. Ten 100-lb. depth charges brought up seven sharks ranging from 3 to 7 feet in length. The two twenty-footers that had been spotted two days before were not in evidence.

The shark nets arrived the same day, January 6, and the Mayor announced that the swimming ban would be lifted as soon as the nets were in position. Forty depth charges in all were let off before the *Vrystaat* left.

Despite the swimming ban, and the intensive publicity surrounding the depth charges, about 100 swimmers had to be ordered out of the surf that day!

On January 9, swimming was not banned in Scottburgh, a town halfway between Karridene, site of the first attack, and Margate. Early that morning (about 7:30), Derick G. Prisloo, 42, his son Jacques, and two old friends, Mr. and Mrs. J. Nieman, ventured into thigh-deep water ten yards from shore. Mrs. Nieman told what happened then:

"Mr. Prinsloo had just been talking to me when he began screaming. I thought it was my husband teasing him by grabbing him from underneath." She then saw the shark clearly. It was about 10 feet in length, and grey in colour. "It did not attack him and leave him—but went on attacking him mercilessly," said Mrs. Nieman.

Another witness, Mrs. Edith Crockett, said:

"The farthest swimmer was about 20 yards out when the attack occurred. Until then no one saw a thing.

"Without any warning at all, there were terrible screams and we saw the flashing black tail of the shark churning the water as it attacked with a circular sweep. The next moment the sea was red with blood."

Brigadier J.T. Durrant, former Director-General of the South African Air Force, was sitting on the beachwall watching his family swim: "Within a minute of their getting out of the surf to swim in the near-by pool I heard a scream from the surf and saw Mr. Prinsloo being attacked.

"I doubt whether he was in 2 ft. of water. Within seconds the sea was dyed with blood.

"He never had a chance. The shark began its attack in 2 ft. of water and ended it with its belly on the sand. When it left him Mr. Prinsloo was only about five yards from the shore."

Prinsloo was unconscious when he was brought out of the water. He died on the way to the hospital.

No one had seen the shark before the attack.

The Scottburgh town board immediately

got in touch with shark-net manufacturers; the first net was placed later in January.

Four hours after Prinsloo's death, there were several hundred vacationers on the beach at Scottburgh. Not one, however, ventured into the ocean.

It was a different story in Durban. There it had been widely publicized that sharks seemed to be attracted to red, yellow, and orange—and that four of the five victims had been wearing these colours. Bob Wherley, who lost a leg at Karridene, wore yellow-striped trunks. Alan Green, who died at Uvongo, wore vivid tangerine shorts; Julia Painting, savaged at Margate, wore a swimsuit with yellow background, and Prinsloo wore dark red.

But "burnt orange" was fashionable that season, and Durban storekeepers reported it was the color most in demand. Despite the fact that Painting was attacked in only four feet of water, Berry was in knee-deep, and Prinsloo in two feet, at least one Durban swimmer remarked, "I'm not scared of sharks. I only dabble on the fringe of the surf."

As January wore on, and shark nets were completed at various points along the coast, more was heard of theories about the attacks. Numerous people seem to have adopted the belief that one "blood-crazed killer" shark was responsible for all the attacks, having developed "a taste" for human flesh. And it was also suggested by the Rev. J.L. von Wielligh that the "wantonness" of the South coast beaches was a cause.

"Will these things, which cry out to Heaven, just continue, and man never be brought to his senses?" he asks.

"In II Kings 17, verse 25, we read of lions which were sent among the idolators. It was terrible to see the South Coast beaches, which at first were so alive, now desolated, yes, a wilderness through which no-one passes.

"One hears everybody talk about the great damage done to business and, of course, to the liquor trade, through many people having packed up and left the area.

"But few showed concern about the damage done to the kingdom of God by all these evils.

"And it is usually the innocent that suffer, because God does not seek the death of a sinner, but that he should repent and be saved."

On a more down-to-earth tack, von Wielligh also referred to the fact that there was a small sardine run that season, probably depriving the sharks of the bigger fish which normally feed on sardines. With fewer fish for the sharks to catch, they would be hungrier than usual.

In March, Professor J.L.B. Smith, an eminent South African shark expert, was quoted in *Veld and Vlei*, a sportsman's magazine, on the probable causes of the attacks:

"One theory is that most attacks have been due to one or two "rogue" sharks. This is possible, though it has been observed that sharks that live inshore, like many other fishes, do not appear to travel widely. They tend to remain in a restricted area, especially when food is available.

"I pointed out early this summer that the flow of the Mozambique current was unusually strong and predicted that larger game fishes, such as tunny and marlin, might well be more abundant than usual along Southern Cape shores. The sea has indeed been abnormally warm, and as most dangerous sharks favor warm seas, conditions this year might well induce them to feed more freely, in addition to favoring the southerly migration of forms normally confined to more tropical zones.

"Dangerous sharks are more abundant in warm seas, and bathing in the open sea and in estuaries in such latitudes is foolhardy. The situation of Natal is unfortunate in this respect. The sea there in summer is warm enough for all tropical sharks to thrive. These creatures normally find food chiefly by smell. They are not only hunters of live prey, such as seals, but feed extensively on offal. From Durban especially there pours out continually with every tide a vast quantity of effluent and offal whose odor must attract great numbers of sharks. Add to this the whaling station, so that we can understand the unusually high concentration of sharks characteristic of Durban seas even in the colder season. This tainted, shark-attracting water is carried along the south coast of Natal, all the growing seaside resorts adding their quota, the crowds of visitors helping to make it worse at the most dangerous time—the summer months. It is no wonder sharks are there in numbers. With so many humans bathing in the sea, tainting it still more, it is surprising that there are not more attacks. Indeed, there are many responsible persons who contend that sharks do not deliberately attack humans, that the relatively few cases occur by chance only."

Whatever the case, the sharks were not through with the south coast.

At the end of March the Easter holiday season began. Immediately swimmers caused official anxiety by flouting safety precautions. Only a few miles south of Margate, a reporter noted a group of teen-agers cavorting in the surf while two youths played what appeared to be a version of "Chicken"—the farthest one out was the "bravest." One of them swam out to at least 50 yards from the shore.

When he remarked to one of the girls that it might be dangerous she merely replied: "That's the idea—otherwise there's no thrill. And anyway, they can take care of themselves. They've got knives in their belts."

"In one morning alone," the reporter continued, "I watched three family groups go into the water. Each time, mother and father and baby would walk down to the surf and bounce baby in the waves while they waded out sometimes to thigh depth. Then father would go back to the beach with baby while mother would swim out into deeper water, sometimes up to shoulder depth."

The south coast mayors were understandably irritated. They were able only to suggest that people swim only in netted areas—there was no law against foolhardiness. And yet, the business of the communities was beach vacations; to have another accident could destroy the towns' economy for a second holiday season.

On April 3, at Port Edward, just south of Margate, 29-year-old Nicolaas Badenhorst was fatally attacked while swimming in chest-deep water some distance from shore. Zepha Masseko started swimming towards Badenhorst, but the shark was so massive (10 feet) he withdrew a little way and waited for the wave to bring the man to him. Badenhorst died in the water.

The next day swimmers were back in the surf at Port Edward.

On April 5, at Uvongo, just north of Margate, Mrs. Fay Bester wore her yellow and red bathing suit down to the beach. With a group of about fifteen others, she went out into knee-deep water to watch the shark nets being repaired. That morning the town had learned that rough seas the night before had wrecked part of the enclosure, and officials had advised all swimmers not to enter the water.

As Mrs. Bester stood and watched, a few paces from the others, a fisherman saw what he called "a silver arrow" flying toward the group. The shark—later estimated at 8 to 9 feet long—tore into Mrs. Bester's stomach. One witness said "it shook her like a dog, and wheeled her half out of the water."

Duncan du Toit, on the beach, heard the crowd shout "Shark!": "I ran towards the woman, and as I reached her the shark was still gripping her. My impression was that there were three or four sharks in the water—I seemed to see fins all round me. I must have reached the woman in a matter of seconds, but I am sure she was dead by that time."

Basil Van Dongen, who was working on the nets, said "I saw the shark throw the woman out of the water, then grab her again. I never heard a scream. It was all too quick."

She was dead when taken from the water.

On April 7 other coastal resorts followed Durban's lead, and put the force of law behind swimming bans.

Mrs. Bester was the last in Natal's hideous five-month string of shark victims.

In 1958 I was at sea, en route from Australia back to the United States, when this series of devastating shark attacks occurred. The Durban City Manager cabled V.M. Coppleson, the Australian shark expert, with whom I had spent my time in Australia, asking for help. The manager was told I would be arriving shortly. Before we entered the channel, the City Manager came aboard and escorted me ashore for a series of meetings, talks, and radio discussions which occupied me completely for the period of my Durban visit. The populace was thoroughly frightened, and a sense of panic pervaded the newspapers. People were almost afraid to get into a tub for a bath.

It was pointed out that at least five victims of the Natal attacks wore bathing suits of the orange-yellow-red color family. Whether color plays a role in attracting sharks has been hotly debated for many years. The recently published Shark Attack: *A Program of Data Reduction and Analysis* concludes: "It is not possible to draw meaningful correlations between incidence of shark attack and colors reportedly worn by victims. But there are considerations other than attack case histories that definitely does point to the probable importance of colors ... in affecting shark behavior.

"To shark researchers, the term "Yum Yum Yellow" stands for International Orange and the related bright yellow and orange-yellow colors ... of life jackets, rafts, etc. These pigments are used ... primarily because they contrast strongly with the background color of ... the sea.... The primary hazard to a man adrift at sea is not shark attack, but is instead the very high probability of not being sighted by search aircraft. ... Unfortunately, ... to be easily seen by one searcher is to be easily seen by all."

Reflectivity is also involved. Ernest B. McFadden of the Federal Aviation Authority remarked to the press after studies of survival equipment in 1971, "Reflectivity is apparently highly attractive to sharks.... They tend to attack any bright object they see in the water." One recommendation arising from that study was to replace chrome elements on survival gear with black, non-reflective material.

As for the shore bather, Shark Attack points out: "The bright, highly reflective dyes ... employed in some swimwear and diving gear for attracting the attention of humans out of the water can be expected to do much the same with sharks when submerged.... Such factors might well come into play in the shark's selection of a particular victim among a group of bathers." At the same time, it is highly unlikely that the shark even sees the color until after visual and olfactory indications have brought him close to hand.

THE
MIDDLE
EAST

PORT SAID, U.A.R.

During the ten years prior to 1899, only two cases of shark attack—one in 1893 and one in 1897, were on record at Port Said. On August 18, 1899, three attacks occurred. The first victime, a 13-year-old Arab boy, was admitted to the hospital at 8:30 a.m. His outer left leg had an enormous wound 10½ inches long. He survived the operation, and was taken home. The second boy, 19 years old, was admitted at 9:30 a.m. He had about a dozen lacerations on the upper right forearm, wrist, and hand, ranging from ½ inch to 3½ inches in length. He survived. The third victim, a boy 9 years old, was admitted at 11:30 a.m. The shark had bitten an oval in his back and under the right arm. Eighty-six stitches were needed. He was discharged on September 2.

All three boys were bathing in the Mediterranean, but not at the same place. None were out of their depth in the water. The danger was not great, since during hot weather hundreds of boys bathed daily along the same stretch of sea. W.B. Orme, who reported the cases to the *British Medical Journal*, thought it likely that one shark was responsible.

THE PERSIAN GULF—
AND 90 MILES
UPRIVER

Ahwaz, a town on the plains of Iran that bestrides the River Karun, lies between oil fields further inland and the oil refineries at Abadan, the Persian Gulf port. Ahwaz is 90 miles from the gulf. Its river, the Karun, flows south to join the Shatt-al-Arab (itself formed by the junction of the Tigris and Euphrates rivers), some 10-20 miles inland from the Gulf. The Shatt-al-Arab flows on to empty into the head of the Gulf.

In the summer of 1941, there was a British military base at Ahwaz, and personnel were stationed along the Shatt-al-Arab as well. Reports of serious injury began coming in—gross lacerations of legs or arms, accompanied by a savage wrenching and convulsing attack by some creature, armed with numerous sharp, inward curving teeth, on swimmers, bathers, and people washing vehicles or equipment at the edge of the water. Some of the latter disappeared.

In 1941 a total of thirteen people were attacked at Ahwaz.

As reported by Lt. Col. R. S. Hunt of the Royal Army Medical Corps, the local records indicated many casualties among the young and the old, mostly undernourished and/or feeble with age. Extremely serious injuries combined with a fatalistic determination to die (it was locally believed that sharks were poisonous) had resulted in a high rate of fatality.

The people of Ahwaz used the river for bathing, and defecating, for washing their clothes, and gathered water in pots for domestic use. They hardly ever went in over ankle depth. The sharks were said to knock people over with their tails; apparently this was not so. In their rush to get out of the water, the victims would slip on the slimy rocks.

The attacks at Ahwaz included the following:

An I.A.S.C. driver backed his ambulance into shallow rocky rapids, and set about washing its rear wheels. He was standing in water less than knee-deep when his right ankle was seized and he was pulled off balance. His right leg was severely injured, and his left hand and forearm lacerated. All tissues were completely stripped from his right arm. He died.

A Gurkha soldier survived, but suffered forequarter amputation.

A boy, 6 years old, slipped off the rocks and was seized by a shark. His mother was filling water pots close by. Both his arms from the wrists down were stripped of flesh. He died.

Hunt reported that he saw an old fisherman in ankle deep water slip and fall as the water in front of him churned. He lay half on his back while the dorsal fin of a shark swirled up and down close by in water stained red by blood. The fisherman's foot was lacerated and crushed. In spite of medical treatment, he "gave up" and died.

Another man, a local dignitary, died twelve days after being attacked; his femoral artery had been cut.

Hunt also saw a Persian soldier fire at a shark, which was plainly visible. People scurried from the water. One small toddler got left behind, and stood, petrified. The shark came near, thrashing its tail, but did not enter the shallows. Had the child moved, he would have slipped and been lost. A man was able to wade in and get him.

One shark caught at Ahwaz was 4 feet, 10

inches long. Its stomach contained fragments of glass bangles.

At Abadan, on the Shatt-al-Arab, there were fewer cases. There the Anglo-Iranian Oil Co. regulated the use of the river. However, there were eleven hospitalized cases of shark attack during 1945-49. Minor lacerations treated in the Out-Patient department of the hospital were not included. A. Anderson, medical officer for Anglo-Iranian in 1950, pointed out that the sharks invaded the Shatt-al-Arab and the Karun during July, August, and September. At that time the fresh-water flow was minimal, and the tidal incursion maximal, with the salt content rising to as much as 500 parts per million.

As at Ahwaz, the victims were mostly in the young and old age groups. Only the young swam in the river waters. The women bathed and washed on the edge of the river with their clothes on; the men used the local baths; the aged bathed and washed in the sea. Here are the cases:

Abdul Karmi, a boy, was attacked on August 19, 1945. One-third of his left leg was amputated. He survived.

Hamid, ——, 13 years old, male, attacked while swimming on Sept. 6, 1945 at Bahmashir. Loss of blood and damage to the flexor and extensor muscles of the right forearm. Mid-humeral amputation. He survived.

Mehdi, ——, 12 years old, male, attacked while swimming at Ahwaz in the Karun on July 18, 1946. His left Achilles tendon was severed, and his calf muscles severely lacerated. He survived.

Khodadad, ——, 12 years old, male, bitten while fishing with a net in the Karun at Dorquain on July 18, 1946. The skin and muscle just below his right elbow were damaged. He survived.

Ali, ——, 38 years old, male, drew a shark in in his net on May 10, 1948. He suffered lacerations and an 8-by-4-inch muscle tear. He survived.

Abdul Hussein, 13 years old, male, was bitten while in the Shatt-al-Arab on August 19, 1948. His right arm was amputated. He had suffered exsanguination. He died fourteen hours after the attack.

Roghai, ——, 60 years old, female, was in the Bandar Ma'shur sea inlet on September 2, 1948, probably bathing or washing. Her left arm was amputated below the axilla, and her left buttock removed. She died twelve hours after the operation.

Abdul Imam, 19 years old, male, was attacked on January 2, 1949. His left thumb was amputated. He survived.

Ismail, ——, 15 years old, male, was attacked while swimming at Bahmashir on August 3, 1948. He suffered lacerations, bad wounds, and a nerve suture in the right arm.

Ali, ——, 18 years old, male, attacked while swimming at Bahmashir. He died two and a half hours after treatment.

R. Palmer, 18 years old, male, a ship's apprentice, was attacked while swimming in the Shatt-al-Arab on September 27, 1949. He had lacerations and a wound in the right leg. He survived.

INDIA

In 1880 and 1881 the Indian Medical Gazette reported three cases of shark bite in the river Hooghly and one in the Ganges. M. N. Ganguli's account of the Hooghly incidents is given in full for the fascinating glimpses it allows into medical practice and social customs in India at the time.

"The unusual prevalence of sharks in the river Hooghly this year has already attracted general attention through some of the local newspapers. Lately I have had three consecutive cases of shark-bite at Panihatty—a place four miles south of Barrackpore and on the river Hooghly.

"*Case* 1.—N——, a boy aged eleven years, went to bathe in the river on the 2nd of May 1880 at about 10 A.M. He was seen struggling some ten cubits off the ghât. Thinking he was being drowned, a neighbouring gentleman went to his rescue, and taking him up to the ghât found him gasping, devoid of the right lower limb, and bleeding from the stump. I was instantly sent for, and I found him dead

137

and the stump quite bloodless. The shark made a transverse section of the right thigh right through the femur, leaving a lacerated stump. He lost all arterial blood through the divided femoral while under the water, and fell dead as soon as he was taken up.

"*Case* 2.—Sasti, a Hindu adult male, shopkeeper by profession, was bitten in his left hand on the same day, at about 12 o'clock noon, within two hours after the first case.

As I was going by boat to an invitation, I heard much *golmal* on the river side. After enquiring into the matter, I landed there and found the man bleeding profusely. There was a deep lacerated wound on the lower half of the anterior aspect of the left forearm, besides a few smaller wounds on the same hand. The radial artery was divided, but the ulnar seemed to be intact. Some of the flexor muscles and tendons were much lacerated, and part of radius and ulna was laid bare. The main bleeding points could not be detected. Having had no pocket-case with me at the time I sent for one from a neighbouring medical man. The patient was taken up and laid under a banyan tree, and with the timely aid of two other medical men I tied the brachial at the middle of the arm without chloroform (because chloroform could not be had then). As there was no catgut or silk ligature in the pocket-case, and no other kind of strong thread at hand, I was obliged to double up a piece of my sacred thread (a Brahmin as I am) and tie the artery thereby, and the bleeding stopped. Although I tied the knot two or three times strongly round the artery, I was fully aware of the weakness of the ligature and consequent chance of secondary hæmorrhage in future. However, under the emergency of the circumstances, I could not help it. I applied a pad of linen just above the ligatured point, one over the distal, and a third over the proximal end of the divided radial after stitching up the wounds, then bandaged up the limb and advised the friends of the patient to take him at once to the hospital. He was admitted into the Second Surgeon's wards, Medical College Hospital, and died there of secondary hæmorrhage after a stay of eleven days.

"*Case* 3.—My third case was an old widow of sixty, of the Brahmin caste.

As she was bathing in the river on the fourteenth (14th) of this month (May), she was bitten by a shark in six places, *viz.*:—

"*Firstly*,—a deep lacerated wound of the

lower third of the anterior aspect of the right forearm, dividing the radial artery about an inch and a half above the wrist, and the flexor carpi radials and flexor sublimis digitorum muscles, lacerating some other muscles and laying bare a part of the radius.

"*Secondly*,—a longitudinal wound on the dorsum of the same hand corresponding to the interspace between the 2nd and 3rd metacarpal bones, dividing the tendon of the extensor longus digitorum for the index finger.

"*Thirdly*,—a superficial wound on the lower part of the anterior aspect of the left forearm, rather to the ulnar side, causing no serious damage to any very important structure.

"*Fourthly*,—two small deep wounds on the dorsum of the left hand corresponding to the first two inter-metacarpal spaces.

"*Fifthly*,—a large lacerated wound on the outer aspect of the middle third of the left thigh about 4 inches by 2½ inches, and nearly one inch deep.

"*Sixthly*,—a large wound of about the same extent on the inner aspect of the upper third of the same thigh; fortunately for the woman, the shark spared the femoral artery, which could be felt distinctly pulsating along the bottom of the wound.

"She bled profusely on the river side, and was very pale and shivering. She was thought to be dying on the spot. However, I had her brought to her home from the river side and tied the cut ends of the right radial artery with carbolised catgut. I then ligatured some other bleeding points and stitched up the gaping wounds, putting a drainage tube into the wound of the anterior aspect of the right forearm. I then applied a splint to each forearm and dressed up all the wounds with carbolic oil (1 in 15), substituting plantain leaf for gutta percha tissue. Besides I have been using decoction of *nim* leaves in place of carbolic lotion. She had fever on the second day, which became higher still on the third. I therefore separated the stitches to prevent bagging of matter. I next gave her a dose of castor oil followed by 20 grains of quinine in four doses (grains 5 each), and she was feverless on the fifth day. Since then I have kept her under a course of iron, quinine and nux vomica, and she has been very rapidly improving. There was, however, a good deal of sloughing and fœtor in the thigh-wounds which rapidly disappeared under strong carbolic oil (1 in 10). All the wounds are healing from the bottom with small red granulations discharging healthy pus. Her bowels quite regular; appetite much improved, and I expect to see her cured within another month.

REMARKS

"My first case was a remarkably uncommon one; I did not hear of a parallel case before. Sharks generally bite, but they very seldom amputate, especially a bulky part like a thigh.

"In my second case, as the main bleeding points could not be detected, the only alternative left was ligature of brachial. I could do it low down at the bend of the elbow, but apprehending any abnormality in point of its bifurcation, I preferred to do it higher. To ligature with sacred thread (made of cotton wool) was unscientific, but I could not help it under the emergency of the circumstances as stated above. As the patient was a robust young man, a primary amputation of the arm might have saved his life.

"The size and number of the wounds, old age, poorly nourished frame and spare and limited diet (because a *Brahmin widow*) are much against her cure. But since she is a *widow*, she has a potent curative agent in her favour, namely, a latent store of vital energy."

Here is the case reported on the Ganges, as told by A. C. Kastagir, the surgeon involved:

"On the 15th May 1880, at 11 A.M., one Haboo *alias* Suttoo Cumar Mukerjea, aged about 20 years, a strong young man full 6½ feet in stature, grand-nephew of an influential native gentleman of Boranogore, named Babu Goluck Chandra Mukerjea, was most seriously bitten by a shark when bathing in the Ganges. The patient having fainted on the spot, I was called to treat him there.

"On examination, I found that the patient's left hand had been completely cut through at the wrist and taken away with two inches of the head of the ulna, and radius broken across. The skin was torn to the extent of 3 inches higher up on the inner aspect of the arm. The skin and soft parts of the calf of the right leg were torn from 2 inches below the knee to 3 inches above the ankle. His pulse was weak, patient having lost a large quantity of blood and just recovered from an attack of syncope. More than 2,000 spectators surrounded the patient.

"There was no time to be lost. After a dose of stimulant, the patient was put under chloroform, and while in the semi-conscious state, the left forearm was amputated 2 inches higher up, leaving the skin flap to cover the stump. It was stitched with sutures and dressed with carbolic dressing.

"A large portion of the skin of the torn leg being disorganised, was removed, and the wound being well washed with strong carbolic lotion, was stitched together with horsehair, and dressed with carbolic oil and bandage.

A full dose of opiate was next given to remove the pain, with which he was suffering much.

"... In eight weeks patient was able to leave his bed, and in four weeks more the wounds completely cicatrized.

"At Panhatty, Barrackpore, Dackhineshwar, Barahonagore, Kashipur, and Chitpore down to Baug Bazar *Ghâts* more than 20 persons have been severely bitten by sharks this year before the setting in of the rains,—all of whom are reported to have died, with the exception of the one herein reported. The success in this case is to be attributed to the promptness of the aid and thorough disinfection of the wound."

NEW
ZEALAND

At St. Clair Beach, Dunedin, New Zealand, on February 5, 1964, Leslie Francis Jordan became the fifth shark fatality in New Zealand's modern history and the first fatality since 1907.

Jordan, a 19-year-old law student, was swimming about 200 yards offshore at 7:30 a.m., having been surfing for about an hour. Sandy McDowell, 19, and Ian Graham, 26, were in the water with him about 50 yards south and slightly farther out. McDowell had just caught a wave and was on his way to the beach when Graham, who had missed the wave, saw that Jordan was in trouble.

"As I paddled toward him," Graham said, "he cried out 'It's a shark!' When I got closer, I said, 'Don't be silly. There are no sharks round here!' I thought he had a cramp.

"He said, 'Have a look at my leg.' When I reached him I saw blood in the water, and his injured leg."

Graham pulled Jordan onto his surfboard, but had to leave his legs in the water because the extra weight was too great for the board.

As they paddled to shore, not making much headway, McDowell arrived to help. Jordan's father, on shore, had seen that the men were in difficulty and had asked McDowell to go back out. McDowell and Graham draped Jordon over the two boards, so that he was completely out of the water, and started off for the shore. It was at this point that McDowell looked back and saw the shark. It was swimming along behind them. He warned Graham to mind his hands while paddling. "I was never so scared as I was then," Graham said.

The shark, which both men said was longer than their 10-foot surfboards, followed them to within 20 yards of the beach, coming within 18 inches of the boards a couple of times.

Jordan was dead on arrival at Dunedin Hospital.

On January 8, 1966, Rae Marion Keightley, 14, was swimming about 20 yards away from 18-year-old Anthony Eric Johns at Oakura Beach, Taranaki, New Zealand. They were 75 to 100 yards offshore when she was struck by a shark. While other swimmers headed for the shore, Johns paddled his surfboard towards her. He saw that a large area of water was bloodstained, and a large brown object swam under his board, bumping it.

On reaching Miss Keightley, he sat on the end of his board and pushed the front part under her. Then, lying over the back of the board, he caught two small waves in towards the shore.

Miss Keightley was dead upon reaching the beach.

Johns was later awarded a gold medal by the Royal Humane Society of New Zealand.

AUSTRALIA

Victor M. Coppleson, known to his close friends as "Cop," was a typical "Aussie"—outgoing, informal, and quick to come to the point. He was a skillful surgeon, and early in his career was associated with one of the many surfing clubs common to Australian bathing resorts. These amateur groups are dedicated to life saving and are composed of good swimmers and small-boat men who compete annually with other groups under their own distinctive colors and insignia. Coppleson's interest in surfing was chiefly medical; the shark-savaged victims brought to him were a challenge to his skill.

In the early 1930's Coppleson was asked to write an account of shark bites for the *Handbook* of the Surf Life Saving Association. For this task he searched the literature back to 1900 for more background and information. These were compiled in his famous report "Shark Attacks in Australian Waters" published in the *Medical Journal of Australia* in 1933. Just 10 years later the same report was lifted from the *Medical Journal* and classified Top Secret by the U.S. Navy in the start of its search for protection from shark attack.

Coppleson was fascinated by shark injuries. He early noted that not all wounds were caused by the teeth; the pectoral fin and head of the shark also cause bodily damage. He was also fascinated by the distribution of the attacks and sought for patterns that might exist in order to ease the danger. He knew little about sharks as a group and depended almost completely on Gilbert Whitley of the Australian Museum for correct identification, proper names, and scientific facts. Coppleson was a strong proponent for the control of sharks by netting of the beaches. He early pointed out that while the risk of shark attacks is small, statistics are no solace; and that shark bites are, in a majority of cases, mortal. Coppleson was knighted after his book *Shark Attack* was published—a tribute to the man who wrote the first book on shark attacks.

Australia has had a history of shark attacks ever since records began to be written down. Between 1933 and 1963, there were, in fact, at least 174 attacks around Australia, including

58 on divers (mainly around the Great Barrier Reef), 65 in New South Wales, 32 in Queensland, 2 in Bass Strait, 4 in Victoria, 3 in South Australia, 5 in Western Australia and 5 in Northern Australia. At the First Intl. Convention on Life-Saving Techniques in 1963, Coppleson pointed out some interesting features of the thirty-year history:

"I think that in any given area, other things being equal, the number of attacks is determined by the number of bathers, the people exposed to attack ... there are more people exposed during the period of danger in Sydney and Newcastle [both in New South Wales] than there are along the Queensland coast. . . .

"The [world-wide] shark attack belt appears to stretch south to about 42° ... and north to about 42° which is just south of Boston in the United States. The belt is divided into a middle tropical zone in which attacks take place all the year round, and southern and northern seasonal zones in which attacks are limited to different times of the year, but appear to occur in accordance with a timetable. . . . There seems little doubt that more attacks occur on east coasts than on west coasts. The reason may be that ... the warm equatorial currents flow from the Equator along east coasts.

". . . Not only are sharks, like most other cold-blooded fishes, affected by warmth, but warmth has a measurable effect on their attack pattern. Once the sea temperature reaches 68 degrees, they tend to become really ferocious. There are a lot of riddles about them I can't understand. Around Sydney for instance they attack for three months of the year. There has never been an attack on a Sydney ocean beach except between January 7 and April 14. But they only attack in Sydney Harbour between Christmas Day and February 7. Why do they confine themselves to Sydney Harbour for six weeks of the year when they attack for three months on the nearby ocean beaches? Perhaps this has something to do with their breeding; it has also been suggested that they are coming in then to teach their young to swim. Whatever it is, it is something which makes them particularly ferocious in inland waters during this period. . . .

"We thus have geographical patterns of attack, temperature patterns and seasonal patterns. There are other patterns which I would like to touch upon also.

". . . Of the attacks around Sydney, this is

what we found. Four attacks took place near Coogee. This is between 1922 and 1925. Then in 1928-1929 there were three attacks within a year at Bondi. No attack had ever been known before at Bondi and that is the last attack at Bondi since 1929. Then between 1934 and 1936, there were five attacks, four of them fatal, along the northern beaches—the long line of beaches from Narrabeen to South Stevne. At this point meshing was introduced and there has never been an attack since this period on any Sydney ocean beach. What ever the explanation of meshing might be it has been proved effective not only here in Australia, but also on the Durban beaches in South Africa.

"The inland waters showed similar patterns. In 1934 there were three attacks in George's River, two of them on the same day, within four hours of each other. In 1940 in Botany Bay a boy was taken at North Brighton. We were then able to predict that unless precautions were taken another attack in the area was likely. Within twelve days a man was killed two hundred yards away from the site of the first attack. The same thing was going on in Sydney Harbour. Here in Middle Harbour a girl was attacked early one year.

Towards the end of that year another girl was attacked within about half a mile. In 1955 an attack occurred at Balmoral and within a few weeks another attack occurred within half a mile. Surely this is a pattern and it is not limited to Australia. I put forward the view, and nobody has attempted to disprove it, that these attacks must be due to one shark, a rogue shark—like a rogue tiger that hangs around and waits—and the attacks will continue until the shark is killed."

Dr. Coppleson had been collecting data on shark attacks for many years. Here are a few of the accounts he related in the *Medical Journal of Australia* in 1933. They suggest the range of times and circumstances in which sharks strike:

At Newcastle beach, on January 18, 1919, at 6:45 p.m., a large shark about twelve to fourteen feet long swam amongst the bathers to within twenty yards of the dry sand and attacked a man. The shark was actually pointed out to him before he entered the water, but he laughed thinking it merely a joke. He dived into the water and a second later was struggling violently and calling for help. It is stated that he was actually torn from the shark's mouth by his rescuers and that while he was being rescued the shark made another snap at him before swimming away.

He was immediately admitted to Newcastle Hospital, where the left leg was amputated at about the knee joint. Four distinct bites were described, three on the left leg near the knee and one on the left hand. By January 20, 1919, his condition had improved and he was discharged on February 17, 1919.

The shark, it is stated, did not give him up without a struggle.

In the Bulimba Reach of the Brisbane River, Queensland, on November 27, 1921, a man was wading out to a dinghy moored about ten yards from the bank, carrying his son, aged eight, on his back. Just before he reached the boat a large shark seized his right hip. He succeeded in beating the shark off, but before he could reach the shore it again attacked, biting his right elbow and forearm and severely lacerating his right wrist. An onlooker on the shore, seeing the fin of the shark, rushed to the injured man's assistance and after a struggle managed to bring him to the bank. The son either fell off the father's back or was pulled off by the shark. The boy's head appeared about five yards away, but only for an instant, and his body was never recovered. The attack took place in three feet of water. The man was immediately taken by a passing police launch to the Brisbane General Hospital, suffering severely from shock. There was a skin wound five inches long on his right buttock, and a severely lacerated wound at the back of the right elbow. He was treated, and was discharged on February 21, 1922.

At Coogee, Sydney, New South Wales, on March 3, 1922, towards 11 a.m., some thirty people were surfing. There was a half-tide. A sandbank running out from an inshore channel furnished a footing for surfers about twenty-five yards from the beach. The foremost of these was a young man, aged twenty-two years. The surf was about knee-deep. The fin of a shark was seen from the shore by the beach inspector making towards the surfers. He immediately gave the shark warning and all made a frantic dash to leave the water, except the young man who, seeing the shark's onslaught, turned to meet it. He punched several times with his right arm at the shark, which took it off, leaving a bleeding stump. He tried to take a small "shoot" in, but again the shark attacked. In the attempt to ward it off he injured his left arm. The two attacks took place within a few seconds. Two men went to his rescue and while they were dragging him in the shark made a third attack. The shock of the impact shook the rescuers. He was conscious on being brought ashore, where he immediately received expert first aid attention. He was then sent to Saint Vincent's Hospital by ambulance, and operated on, but by midnight gas gangrene had set in. He died at 5 p.m. on March 4.

The beach inspector, who saw the shark, described it as a blue pointer about eight feet long.

At Pialba Beach, between Scarness and Torquay, Maryborough, on December 5, 1922, a young man, aged nineteen years, was bathing with three friends during a very high tide in about three or four feet of water, when he was attacked from the shore side by a shark, which appeared to be about nine feet in length. A friend went to his assistance and rescued him. The right side of his chest wall was badly torn and below that a complete bite extending from the lower ribs, including the tissues of the right hip, had been taken out, the teeth having apparently slipped down from the chest wall in the struggle. He died about one minute after rescue.

The shark continued to swim around and was easily seen from the shore. It was described as a "blue shark." Several lines were put out and some shots were fired at it, but without effect. Prior to the attack, there were a lot of mullet in the water and a large shark had been seen in the vicinity. This was the first attack known to have occurred on this beach for forty years.

At Coogee Sydney Harbour, New South Wales, on March 27, 1925, a boy, aged sixteen years, was bathing at 5:30 p.m. in foam-spattered surf and in shallow water about twenty to thirty yards from the shore. He was up to about his waist in the water when he was attacked by a shark. Onlookers who saw the shark stated that it was small. The shark bell was rung before the attack took place. It is said that the shark leapt from the water and turned over to bit him, first above the knee and then below, but was unable to drag him into deep water, lashing the sea furiously in an attempt to do so. The young man broke away and staggered to the shore; the shark in the meantime swam off. He was taken by ambulance to Saint Vincent's Hospital. The following notes are taken from the hospital records.

The patient was admitted about 6 p.m. on March 27, 1925, with a history of shark bite on the left leg. He was very shocked, pale and sweating; he was conscious and in great pain. On examination the left leg had a tourniquet above the injuries, which consisted of a deep gash down to the bone in the middle third of the left thigh laterally, and numerous jagged gashes down the leg. The tibia was exposed above the ankle. The middle third of the lower leg was bandaged and left so until operation. The temperature was subnormal.

Operation was performed at 9 p.m. by Dr. Edye. Blood transfusion of 700 cubic centimetres was given at 11 p.m. The patient's condition picked up considerably after this. On operating a deep gash down to the bone was found on the lateral side of the left thigh and below that there were many severe lacerations down to the ankle. The fibula was fractured, the tibia indented and the knee joint widely opened. All the wounds were full of sand. Amputation was performed at the junction of the upper two-fifths and lower three-fifths of the thigh; the wounds healed well and the patient was discharged on May 4, 1925.

The wounds in this case are of considerable interest. It is difficult to understand from the configuration of a shark's jaws how deep and almost straight incised wounds could be caused by their bite. The patient himself definitely stated that he was attacked twice.

At Port Hacking, New South Wales, on January 4, 1927, a young man, aged fifteen years, was bathing with a crowd of others at Grey's Point about 11:30 a.m. Suddenly the fin of a large shark appeared several yards away. It disappeared and a few seconds later the bathers heard the boy call out. The shark had seized his leg, and struggling frantically, he was dragged beneath the surface. His head and chest appeared shortly afterwards several yards away from the spot where he had first been seized. The crowd of bathers realized that the shark was dragging him into deep water. Several swimmers went to his rescue. The shark was holding tenaciously to his leg and for several seconds one of his rescuers punched it with all his strength. Suddenly both of them disappeared and when they rose to the surface it was evident that the shark had released its hold. The rescuer was bringing the boy in when the shark made another attack, but was beaten off. A rowing boat picked them up. As an eye-witness stated, "this fact explodes the theory that a swimmer is safe from sharks amongst a crowd."

The flesh of one leg had been torn completely off, except for a small strip, from the thigh to the ankle, leaving the bones exposed, also "teeth marks" about the boy's body.

He was taken to St. George Hospital by ambulance, but was dead before arrival. The shark remained in the vicinity for some time and was said to have been about twelve feet in length. . . .

At Merewether Beach, New South Wales, on March 1, 1927, a boy, aged seventeen years, was attacked by a shark. According to the story of his rescuer, they were "waiting for shoots" about fifty yards from the beach, when suddenly the boy shouted, "help, help"! and thrashed the water wildly with his hands. The surf was tinged with blood. They both came in together on a shoot for about twenty yards. The rescuer supported him and helped him in until later other assistance came.

Onlookers stated that the first bite was on the thigh, and as he turned for an instant to catch a "shoot", the shark attacked him again with lightning rapidity. It is thought that while trying to ward off the second onslaught he lost his thumb.

He was taken to the club room and later to the Beach Hotel, where first aid was rendered. The ambulance soon afterwards took him to Newcastle Hospital in a critical condition.

He was one of the best junior swimmers of the Merewether Club. The shark, which was said to have been a grey nurse, was later seen to be cruising up and down the shore about fifty or sixty yards from the beach.

Notes received from Dr. Rock, the Superintendent of New Castle Hospital, are that he was admitted at 5 p.m. on March 1, 1927. His right thumb had been bitten off at the base and practically the whole of his right buttock was gone, including most of the gluteal muscles. This wound was about the size of a large dinner plate, and there were also two or three tooth marks on the medial side of the left buttock. In addition, he had a wound about the size of a soup plate higher up on the same side. This was more or less superficial, except in one place where the sacrum was bared. Several skin grafts were necessary.

The boy recovered to walk without a limp.

At Cook's Hill, New South Wales, on April 4, 1928, there was a sandbank about fifty yards from the shore. A man went for a swim about 6 p.m. with two young women, who entered the water first. He swam out to the sandbank, where the water was a little over his waist. Suddenly he threw up his arms and shouted: "Help! A shark has got me!" The water was seen to be tinged with blood. One of the women went for help; the other very courageously went to his assistance. He attempted to beat the shark off with his hands, but was attacked again and again. The woman, by splashing the water vigorously, evidently frightened the shark. She had great difficulty in bringing him ashore, until assisted later by two Cook's Hill lifesavers.

He was immediately taken by ambulance to the Newcastle Hospital, but died before arrival. His rescuer stated at the inquest that she felt his pulse in the ambulance and it was then beating. Notes from the Newcastle Hospital are that he "was dead on arrival in casualty about 6 p.m. on April 4, 1928. There was a very large laceration on the outer side of his right thigh, just below the hip joint, extending almost down to bone, and several superficial lacerations all down the front of both legs. His right hand was amputated at the wrist as cleanly as though done with a saw."

At Bondi, Sydney Harbour, New South Wales, on April 14, 1928, a boy, aged nineteen years, was swimming at about 4 p.m. waiting for "shoots" with a number of other swimmers about a hundred yards from the shore. They all "got the wave" except this boy who was treading water alone when he was attacked and dragged several yards under water. Although the flesh was stripped from knee to ankle on one leg, he swam nearly a hundred yards unaided.

In an interview given to the *Sydney Morning Herald* he stated: "I felt like a sharp stab of pain in my leg as the shark got me in its jaws. Then I went under and tried to beat it off with my fist. I punched it several times, where, I don't know. I think it was on the jaw but it had me in a vise-like grip. Finally I succeeded and in a flash I was free. My leg was not hurting me much; it seemed numb."

On reaching shore, he was quickly taken to the club house, where a tourniquet was applied. He was taken by ambulance to Saint Vincent's Hospital. The hospital record gave the following description of his injuries and his progress.

He was admitted on April 14, 1928. The whole of the left leg from just below the knee to the ankle was stripped of soft tissues. The fibula was missing and the tibia was eaten away to some extent. A ligature was present above the knee (tourniquet): the patient was conscious. He was very shocked on admission, pulseless and cyanosed. . . . His condition then improved slightly and he was taken to the operating theater at 7 p.m. . . . His pulse was now palpable, its rate being 120. Operation started at 7:55 p.m. and lasted until 9:15 p.m. Blood transfusions were given; his general condition improved to such an extent that Dr. Edye decided to amputate. Amputation was performed three inches above the knee. . . .

The patient was returned to the ward in fair condition. He was discharged on May 14, 1928.

At Alma Bay, near Magnetic Island, Townsville, on January 27, 1929, a young man, aged eighteen years, was swimming at about 5:30 p.m. The tide was low, and there were about forty people bathing at the time, and at least six bathers were beyond him. Suddenly he was seen to be struggling violently. A shark had seized him by the left arm, which it took off above the elbow. It attacked again, inflicting a large gash on his right buttock. In a third attack, his right forearm was taken off. He walked ashore and a nurse who was present rendered first aid. He was taken by launch to Townsville, where he was admitted to hospital. He was conscious throughout. At hospital, he was operated on and both arms were amputated, one above, the other below the elbow. He became unconscious at 10 p.m., and died at midnight.

In the Parramatta River, Sydney Harbour, New South Wales, on December 26, 1929, a boy, aged sixteen years, went for a swim in White Bay, near Bald Rock Jetty. He dived in and rose to the surface shouting "Shark!" The water was tinged with blood. Onlookers saw a long grey shark attack him again and again. It then cruised around him until a motor boat arrived. The shark is said to have swum around and round, snapping at the boy every few seconds. When he was lifted on board the launch it was found that his left arm was amputated above the elbow and there were lacerations on his chest. The thumb of his right hand was missing, and there were abrasions where the rough hide of the shark had brushed past him, and a jagged wound of the left thigh, extending down to the bone.

The attack occurred about twenty yards

from the wharf. The ambulance was soon on the spot, but the boy died soon after being rescued. The water temperature at this site was about 21.1°C. (70°F.) on the day of the attack.

At Encounter Bay, South Australia, on March 6, 1931, a young fisherman was hauling in a net when he discovered that it contained a "cocktail" shark, about six feet long. He had pulled it into the boat and was disentangling the net when the shark snapped at his hand and gripped it. The man gouged at the eyes of the shark with his other hand and it then released its hold. The second finger of his right hand was badly bitten and two others lacerated. Owing to weakness and loss of blood he was unable to control the boat, which drifted until he was rescued by another fisherman.

At Kissing Point, Townsville, Queensland, on January 4, 1933, a man and a boy went for a swim off the beach. The boy was sitting in three feet of water, when he saw the grey form of a shark shoot through the water. He hastily ran ashore, calling to the man to hurry out. On reaching the shore he saw the man struggling on his knees and the water reddened with blood. The shark swam away and the boy rushed to the man, who was dead and frightfully mutilated about the body. A shark was known to have been in the vicinity. Fourteen days previously, a man leaving the water's edge, heard a scuffle behind him and turned round to see his dog bitten in two by a large shark.

TWO
FINAL
ODDITIES

ATTACKS ON BOATS

It strains credulity that sharks can and do attack boats, but such is indeed the case.

The literature contains many reliable eyewitness accounts of sharks repeatedly and deliberately "bumping" boats and life rafts as well as swimmers. Well-documented records also describe their savage assaults on boats, oars, and other objects trailed overside. In almost all instances the culprits are the open-sea, swift and wide-ranging species so often associated with human attacks. Unlike the large and small whales whose flukes have been known to crush boats, sharks, even the long-tailed thresher sharks, are not known to use their tails in defense or attack.

The great basking sharks laze on the sea's surface, often lying in busy shipping lanes. On frequent occasions ships have run into them. The smaller the ship, the greater the shark— at least to the captain, who is often convinced that he has struck an unmarked reef or another ship. Probably many basking sharks have been badly injured or killed unknown to the crews of heavy, swift vessels.

In a personal communication to me, Ivan E. Walenta, at the time a Senior Research Engineer for C.I.T.'s Jet Propulsion Laboratory, relates his own experience of shark attack on a boat:

"On August 31, 1958 three other people and I were fishing in the coastal waters off Ensenada, Baja California, Mexico. We were in a sixteen foot cabin cruiser with a 35 horsepower outboard motor. The electric pump for our bait tank failed just outside the harbor so we stopped the motor to make repairs on the electric pump. While stopped, a hammerhead shark of approximately seven-foot length made two passes each at the boat and at the propellor of the outboard motor. He bumped the boat with his nose twice and twice tried to take the propellor in his mouth. Each time we turned over the propellor with the boat starter and the shark veered off, only to return. After being scared off after the second attempt to mouth the propellor he described several circles about the boat.... His dorsal fin was out of the water about six inches and he circled at a distance of about 20 feet. He began another pass at the boat motor but we started the motor at the instant, having completed our repairs. The time was about 7:15 in the morning and there was light fog reducing visibility to one half mile. We returned to the spot about 3:00 in the afternoon and found water skiers in the area but they paid no attention to our warnings, even though one of the boat passengers was an ex-commercial fisherman who warned them that the shark was dangerous.

"Estimate of shark length was obtained by comparison with the cockpit of the boat, which is seven feet long. The shark was almost this precise length. The shark was scarred on his right side with one scar an inch wide, pointed on both ends, running diagonally from a spot just forward to his dorsal fin back down toward his belly. The scar was about 12 inches long. There were a multiplicity of smaller scars surrounding the larger one. The shark's passes were quite slow and unhurried although the impact against the boat and motor was considerable. I hesitate to judge his weight, having nothing to compare against."

THE LAST WORD

Even a dead shark is not harmless.

On Feb. 14, 1927, the U.S.S. *Borie* was in Salinas Bay, Nicaragua. A shark was caught, and its head severed from its body. While the head was suspended from the anchor davit, a sailor began feeling the teeth. Suddenly the jaws closed, causing wounds of the right hand. The artery leading to the index finger was severed; the wound was one inch long by ¼ inch deep.

ADVICE TO THOSE IN SHARK-INFESTED WATERS

The Shark Research Panel affiliated with the American Institute of Biological Sciences and under the auspices of the Office of Naval Research included Stewart Springer, one of the most observant students of shark ways, and one of the best informed, most conservative specialists. The Panel's contribution to shark information was the publication *Sharks and Survival* and the continuation of Coppleson's shark attack listing, renamed the International Shark Attack File. The program of data reduction and analysis based on the file is also an extension of Coppleson's ideas. The difference lies in the larger number of samples and the use of sophisticated computer analysis. The statistical gain doesn't provide ultimate solutions, however.

One fact is indisputably clear: With an increasing interest in water sports, and particularly scuba diving, shark incidents will persist. With more effective communications, reports will improve. One consequence will be more data, but whether these can be statistically meaningful for answers on how best to protect humans from shark attack remains to be seen. Casualties tend to become statistics.

There is no lack for advice to bathers, including information specially prepared by the military for use by the armed forces. Opinions vary, and statistical analysis has contributed little to increase the safety factor. However, there are common-sense rules, such as those proposed by Coppleson based on his research on Australian attacks. You can also draw your own conclusions from the case histories reported in this book, and make up your own set of rules. Basically:

Don't bathe on unfamiliar or lonely beaches.

Avoid beaches where shark attacks have occurred.

If there is a shark alarm clear out of the water; investigate and record shark appearances for credibility.

There is some safety in numbers, so keep to groups.

Don't swim far off shore.

Swim in clear water where you can see anything unusual and thus avoid a possible accidental encounter. Avoid muddy water or swimming at night. Lack of vision is no disadvantage to a shark. Avoid *culs-de-sac* and deep drop-offs.

When swimming from a boat, look before you leap. Be particularly careful of entering the water, or trailing hands or feet over the side of the boat, if you have been cleaning fish over the side.

Blood, vomit, excrement, even urine released in water are suspected of attracting sharks.

In Sydney Harbour, the absence of a pet dog was often the first indication of the presence of a hungry shark. Avoid swimming with animals in the water. One of the oddest cases reported on the West Coast of Africa was a successful attack by sharks on an elephant fording the water between an island and the mainland.

When surfing, keep an eye out for unusual shadows in the water.

Bright colors, flashing sunlight on shiny ornaments, or lightly tanned feet and arms may possibly serve as lures to curious sharks.

Divers are always taking a risk when swimming alone. Even the presence of a companion is no deterrent to shark attack. However, the assistance rendered by a companion may make all the difference between life and death.

Spearfishing draws sharks, and the speared

fish acts as an attractant advertising a source of food.

There is varying opinion on the best protective coloration for wetsuits. Yellow—sometimes referred to as "Yum Yum Yellow"—appears suspect.

In the event of a shark sighting, clear out of the water as quietly as circumstances permit.

Don't tease or play with sharks in any circumstances whatsoever. Small sharks have sharp teeth and can sever muscles or a tendon.

Limit your ocean activities to daylight. In the event of an attack you will need every advantage.

IF YOU ARE ATTACKED

Keep close to your companions.

Swim smoothly in retreating.

Repel attacks with whatever weapons you have handy.

Go for its eyes and its gills rather than its nose.

Keep your eye on the shark.

IF YOUR COMPANION IS ATTACKED, WHAT SHOULD YOU DO?

Very early in his Australian studies, Coppleson observed that in an attack a shark becomes so obsessed with its victim that it will disregard other bathers nearby. There are well-recorded incidents of this trait among sharks. The attack on Barry Wilson described in this book is a good example. The International Shark Attack File shows that in 270 cases of in-water rescue of shark victims, only three rescuers were reported killed, although others were slightly injured. Why this should be the case, no one knows. While reviewing the North American incidents in 1954, I came to recognize this fact. But even so, and with the statistical reassurance of the International Shark Attack File, I wonder what I would do in such a situation.

It remains a question.

FIRST AID FOR VICTIMS

Bleeding requires emergency action and should be controlled as soon as the victim is taken from the sea, if not done while in the water.

Preserve severed members when the opportunity is there, since these may sometimes be restored by surgery.

The victim should be gotten to a physician as quickly as possible—even if the injury appears slight.

ABOUT THE AUTHOR

George A. Llano was born in Cuba in 1911. He received his B.S. degree in icthyology from Cornell University and his M.S. in Museum Education from Columbia University. While serving in the U.S. Air Force (1943-46), he was asked to test a solar still under survival conditions. His life raft got away from the PT boat tending him, and he was lost for three days in the Atlantic Ocean. He saw sharks continually, but was not attacked.

After the war Dr. Llano studied at Uppsala University before receiving his Ph.D. in botany from Washington University, St. Louis, in 1948. After serving as Curator of Cryptograms at the Smithsonian Institution, Associate Professor at the Air University, Maxwell Air Force Base, Alabama, and Science Specialist for the Library of Congress, Dr. Llano joined the Office of Polar Programs, National Science Foundation, where he is now Chief Scientist.

In addition to *Sharks: Attacks on Man* and *Airmen Against the Sea*, Dr. Llano is the author of "Open-Ocean Shark Attacks," in *Sharks and Survival*, and the articles on "Sharks" and "Chondrichthyes" in the *Encyclopedia Britannica*, among numerous other articles. He is co-editor of the U.S. Air Force *Survival Manual*.

Dr. Llano and his wife, the parents of three children, live in the suburbs of Washington, D.C.

HI-RISE BOOK CASES
THE ANSWER TO YOUR
PAPER BACK BOOK
STORAGE PROBLEM

Exclusive thumb cut
for easy book removal

**Your Paper Back Books Deserve a Good
Home Free From Dust, Dirt and Dogears.**

Save shelf space; keep paper back books attractively stored, dust-proof, readily accessible.

- All-new Storage Case with handsome, padded leatherette covering complements any room decor, stores approximately 15 books compactly, attractively.
- Shelves tilted back to prevent books from falling out.
- Handsome outer case elegantly embossed in gold leaf — choice of 4 decorator colors: black brown green red.
- Gold transfer foil slip enclosed for quick 'n easy personalization.